This is a work of fiction. Names, characters, places, and incidents are either the product of the author's imagination or are used fictitiously. Any resemblance to actual events, places, organizations, or persons, living or dead, is entirely coincidental.

First Printing February 2006
WAGER OF SIN
Copyright © 2006 by JESS MICHAELS
ISBN: 1-59836-100-7
Cover art and design © 2006 by D. L. Taylor

For information, you can find us on the web at
www.VenusPress.com
PO Box 584 Hillsborough, NC 27278

WAGER OF SIN

By

Jess Michaels

Venus Press LLC

Jess Michaels

Dedication:

For everyone who encouraged me to continue pursuing Hawk and Bianca's story, but especially Susanna Carr, whose voice of support is often the loudest. And for Michael, because he makes every day my own personal 'happily ever after'.

Chapter One

London, Summer 1817

Hawk barely stifled a yawn. These parties were such God-awful boring events. He would much rather have been at home enjoying a brandy. Or better yet, a woman. Instead…

He sighed as he looked around at the horde of debutantes who had surrounded him from the moment he dared cease moving. They were all pretty girls, but they were looking to tame a rake. To teach a rogue to be a puppet for them and Hawk wouldn't have it. He wasn't interested in their so-called feminine wiles or their irritating need to set traps and demand compliments. He would tell the bunch of them to go to hell if it wasn't guaranteed to start a riot where he would surely be called out by a dozen angry brothers and fathers.

"Do you, Mr. Hawkins?"

Hawk shook his head and forced himself to focus. "I beg your pardon?"

One of the young women in his harem cocked her head and batted her long eyelashes. Her lower lip eased into what would have been a tempting pout if it weren't so average, but her beauty was lost on Hawk as the crowd around them began to stir. A rumble went through the people. A hiss of whispers and a shuffle of skirts that made Hawk's attention prick and his body stiffen with awareness.

Bianca.

Only Bianca caused a commotion like that.

With a pivot on his heel, Hawk strode away from the debutante who was still yammering in mid-sentence. He elbowed his way through the crowd until he reached the large, open entryway to the ballroom.

Sure enough, there was Bianca Clairemont on the arm of her latest lover, Everett Firth. She was dazzling with her slender figure and the air of confidence that hung around her in a way considered unladylike. Hawk found it fascinating.

On the other hand, Firth was tall and thin, with a bird-like nose and no real outstanding features one way or another. Why Bianca had wasted her ample charms on Firth for the last few months was a mystery to Hawk.

"I cannot believe it," a female voice hissed behind him. Her whisper was meant to carry, not hush her words. "Why would Lady Langley invite a fallen woman such as Bianca Clairemont to her soirée? Even if she *was* once Lady Penfry?"

A second woman laughed. "My dear, it is only because she was Lady Penfry and *is* the Earl of Covey's daughter that she has any allowance into society at all. She's an absolute hoyden, you know. She's a half step away from being a common-"

Hawk turned on the gossiping biddies and arched his famous dark brow. The middle-aged matrons both blushed as bright as schoolgirls before they scattered into the crowd out of his sight. With a smile, he turned back to Bianca.

She was wearing a blue gown, not quite the vivid color of her eyes, but as close as the dyers could be expected to achieve. It swept down in a low, round neckline to reveal the delectable top slope of her breasts and a hint of the sweet valley between. A gray ribbon was tied beneath, lifting the globes as if in offering. How Hawk wished he could take that offering. Bury himself between them until she moaned. Then he'd pull the mother-of-pearl pins out of her blue-black hair and let the wave of it cascade over him. Drown him.

Only he couldn't.

With a frown, he adjusted subtly to relieve the pressure on his now swollen cock. Bianca was a treasure he couldn't taste. No matter how much he wanted to sample the sweetness of her lush body.

But he could watch her and did as she released Firth's arm and glided forward on her own. By the wicked turn of her lips, it was clear she was aware of being center of attention. As she passed, the men drew nearer like flies to the sweetest honey and the women actually turned jade with jealousy. They all hated her. Like the women behind him, they believed she was one step away from… From what?

Hawk's smile broadened. Bianca was one step away from so very many things. His bed for one. Or so it seemed sometimes by the way she presented herself to him so provocatively.

Her gaze swept over the crowd in one smooth movement and immediately she caught sight of him. Her coral pink lips swept back in a wide, unladylike grin. One that sent blood rushing back to his groin as she strolled his way.

Hawk straightened and readied himself for the storm that was Bianca. His gambling partner. His obsession. The widow of his late best friend.

His smile turned to a frown. That last one always took the heat out of his erection.

"There you are." As Bianca reached his side, she tapped his arm with her fan in a playful gesture. Light danced in her eyes and desire. Always desire.

He wanted to be triumphant when he saw that need in her. To know she could have, and had had so many other men, but wanted him. Only it didn't. Not after what had happened to her husband.

He shrugged off his thoughts and put on his very best dashing persona. "Bianca, I didn't notice you arrive."

She threw back her head and laughed, filling the air around them with the husky sound. Hawk fought the urge to close his eyes and simply enjoy it. With careful control, he was able to remain passive.

Bianca's laughter faded into a genuine smile. "Hawk, you naughty man, don't lie to me. I saw you watching me all the way from the door." With a wink, she leaned closer and allowed Hawk a brief whiff of her scent. Wild like rainwater on heather. Her voice dropped one level. "I was melting from it."

Hawk swallowed hard. Bianca was teasing him, playing as she always did, but God help him, her words affected him. If he had his way, he would drop to his knees right this very moment, flip up her skirts and taste her for the whole damned *ton* to see. Consequences, gossip and propriety be damned.

Instead, he shook his head and played along. "I doubt that."

For a brief moment, he thought he saw real emotion play across Bianca's face. From time to time he caught those glimpses of the real woman beneath the playful, sensual mask. But they were fleeting. Gone before he could savor them.

"But I did save you from that hideous gaggle of grasping debutantes, didn't I? Don't I deserve some kind of reward for that?" She batted her long, dark eyelashes.

Hawk looked down at her and lost himself in her eyes for just the briefest moment. A long string of fantasies danced before his face at her suggestive comment. An image of him kissing her, stripping her of all the layers of gown and underskirt until she lay naked on his bed and then taking her. Letting his cock slide into her inch by inch until she pulsated around him wildly.

"Hawk?" She wrinkled her brow. "Are you even attending?"

He swallowed hard and somehow managed to keep a precarious rein on control. He gave her a dry smile and said, "When we next play cards, I shall give you a hand for free as a reward, how about that?"

She pursed her lips. "Oh, damn. I had hoped you might forgive all my vowels to you."

Hawk tilted his chin back and let out a long, loud burst of laughter. He was vaguely aware of the female heads that pivoted in his direction at the sound, but was too focused on Bianca to care. "You would need to save me from a ravenous pack of lions to make me forget the entirety of your debt. A hand at cards is far too generous as it is."

Bianca's mouth twitched around the corners and a dimple appeared in her cheek as she took a breath in preparation to retort. Before she could say whatever wicked thing was on her mind, Hawk caught a glimpse of her father coming from the corner of his eye. Her father and two of her three brothers. All three looked more than a little pissed.

"Brace yourself," he whispered as he motioned his head in their direction.

She peeked over her shoulder and grimaced, just as her father reached her elbow.

"Bianca." Lord Covey said as he folded his arms in a pose of utmost displeasure. While the older gentleman concentrated on his daughter, Bianca's brothers both focused entirely on Hawk.

"Papa." Bianca smiled as if she couldn't have been happier to see her father.

Her lie seemed convincing, but Hawk knew better. Their relationship had been strained even before her husband, Oscar's death, though he didn't know the cause of the rift.

"I didn't know any of you would be here. What a nice surprise." She pressed a kiss against her father's wrinkled cheek, but the man wouldn't be deterred by her considerable acting skills.

"Come with me," he said in a low voice filled with warning.

She laughed, but again Hawk saw that fleeting flash of emotion. This time he identified it as frustration, anger and even a little fear. "You are being abominably rude, Father. Can't you see I am in the middle of something with Hawk–Mr. Hawkins, here?"

Lord Covey turned his gaze on Hawk and sniffed with distain. Hawk returned his glare with a cool smile, but never turned away from Bianca's two menacing brothers. "My lord."

Covey ignored his greeting. "*Now*, Bianca."

Bianca rolled her eyes toward Hawk, as if they were in this together, then took her father's arm. "Yes, Papa, of course."

The moment they were out of sight, Bianca's eldest brother, Henry Renfire glared at Hawk. "Don't think I am not aware of what you are attempting."

Hawk masked a smile while he kept an eye on the folded-armed Philip Renfire. "Attempting, my lord? I was simply having a civil conversation with your sister. One *she* initiated, I might add." He pressed a hand to his chest as if offended. "I certainly wouldn't be so rude as to snub a lady. That would be grounds for calling me out, would it not?"

Henry pushed up on him, invading Hawk's space despite being a few inches shorter and not nearly as strong. Hawk had to admire him for his balls. Not only was he willing to tangle with a larger man, but he was willing to make a scene in a public place. Obviously Bianca's family was more worried about her than she knew.

"Just leave her be. She has enough problems without you pulling her back into that depraved existence her so-called husband created. I can only imagine the life you would have for her would be far worse."

Hawk arched an eyebrow as Henry gave him a rough push, then he and his brother stormed off into the crowd.

With a sigh, Hawk ignored the pointed stares of those who had overheard the argument and headed for the nearest tray of drinks. As he downed a glass of champagne in one gulp, he contemplated what Henry Renfire had said.

Hawk could only imagine the life he would create for Bianca, too. And sensuality would only be the beginning of the pleasures they shared.

* * *

"Papa, there's no need to drag me across the room." Bianca gave her father's arm a gentle squeeze as she struggled to keep up with his long strides. "I doubt Hawk will pursue me. Especially with Henry and Philip attacking him at your orders."

She tossed a glance over her shoulders and was proven right. Hawk was surrounded by her two brothers, but he looked bored rather than menaced. His gray eyes never revealed his emotions and every dark hair was perfectly in place. He was as beautiful as always and even across a room, he made her heart leap.

Her father stopped at the edge of the dance floor to face her. His entire demeanor was full of painful disapproval. Bianca had gotten used to that look in the last few years, but it never ceased to cause her pain and a flash of anger. Still, she longed for the days when his smile was full of pride. She simply wasn't willing to pay the price for his support. Not when her father had created the life she now lived through his decisions.

"I wouldn't put it past *Mr. Hawkins* to do just that, even if all three of your brothers were holding him back by force."

Bianca sighed. She felt the same old arguments coming on and the thought exhausted her before they'd even begun. "Oh, Papa."

He led her to a quiet corner, away from the throng and their listening ears. Placing one hand on each of her barely clad shoulders, he said, "You're only hurting yourself with your behavior. Please abandon your wild ways and come home to your family."

Clenching her teeth, she said, "You were the one who sent me away from my home and family when you arranged my marriage. If you do not like how that marriage changed me, I hardly think you can put the blame entirely on my shoulders."

His face darkened. How he hated to be reminded of that truth.

His voice dropped lower. "I never thought your marriage would be as it was, Bianca. But now that Oscar is long dead, you don't have to continue down the path he made for you. You can come home."

She rolled her eyes discreetly. It seemed they had this conversation weekly now. Her father had made it more than clear that he didn't approve of the sensual life she'd lead with her husband, Oscar Clairemont. And he was even less pleased with the way she had behaved since Oscar's tragic death. She had taken her husband's generous inheritance and the unheard of freedom he gave her in his last will and gone on living their decadent life. Her string of lovers had been legendary and often public.

Why shouldn't she live as she pleased? She had learned well from her marriage that no one could protect her but herself. So she lived for pleasure and the control her lifestyle afforded her. Over her own emotions and over the relationships she kept. Never again would she allow a man to determine her fate.

If she did as her father asked, she would be dragged back to the staid, bound life she lead before she was liberated. Her father would be free to choose another husband for her, another future in which she had no say.

She tilted her head as she reined in her anger. "Papa, we cannot continue to have the same argument over and over. You already know my answer."

His lips thinned into a sad frown that touched her, even when she tried to remain immune. "I know more than that, Bianca."

"More?"

"I know you've been gambling in the-" He bit off the sentence as if it tasted rotten. "In the hells."

Bianca's heart leapt. Though her comings and goings were often the topic of vicious gossip, her gambling habits were much more secretive. Mostly because the men who saw her gamble didn't want to admit they, too, had been indulging in the debauched underground of the hells.

And yet her father knew.

"Where did you hear that?" she asked, careful to keep her tone neutral and even amused. She would not lie to her father to hide her life as if she was ashamed, but she could mislead him with omissions and unspoken denials.

Her father's eyes narrowed. "Your brothers saw you there."

For a moment Bianca could only stare in stunned silence, but then she shrugged away from his touch and let out a sarcastic laugh. Nothing ever changed. "And were you horrified to learn the three of them were wiling away the hours in the evils of the hells?"

Her father's nostrils flared at her defiant tone, but he gave no answer.

"No, of course you weren't. Because it is expected that they do some carousing and wild play. Why am I expected to live up to different standards than the ones you hold them to?"

"Because you are my daughter!"

Her father's loud tone startled her and drew the attention of several nearby guests. Alan Renfire scowled at the people who dared stare, then drew Bianca even further away from the crowd.

He ground his teeth and repeated himself in a much lower tone. "You are my daughter and I know you aren't faring well. I know you've been playing with your *'friend'* Hawkins. And you've been losing."

Bianca shrugged. Somehow when she played with Hawk, winning and losing didn't matter very much. She got far too caught up in their playful banter and the undercurrent of powerful sexual attraction that sparked between them. Days often went by before she fully realized how much she'd lost to him. Yet even when her inheritance dropped significantly after each game, she never quite felt sorry.

She decided to simply tell as much of the truth as was prudent. "Hawk doesn't cheat. He's a perfect gentleman."

"Lucius Hawkins doesn't know the meaning of the word." Her father's voice went up again and a few more heads turned in their direction.

Bianca shook her head. This had to stop before her father had an apoplexy. "Papa, I won't talk to you about Hawk or any other man I spend time with. You gave up the right to determine my actions and my fate when you sent me into marriage with Oscar. I am who I am because of that decision. I shall not change what I have become. Not for you. Not for anyone." Ignoring the hurt and angry expression on his face, Bianca reached up to pat his wrinkled cheek. She didn't hate him. In fact, she loved him deeply. But he didn't understand and he never had. "Excuse me. I'm sure Everett is looking for me."

She turned away to go, but the iron grip of her father's hand on her elbow stopped her short. Shocked, Bianca looked down at the fingers he had curled around her arm. He hadn't grabbed her so harshly in her entire life. And he'd never looked at her with such wild desperation, either.

"If you refuse to see reason on your own accord, I can force you."

The blood slowly drained from Bianca's face as she shook her father's hand from her arm and rubbed the red mark where he had gripped her. A threat? So it had come to this.

She drew in a calming breath and forced a smile. "You could force me, but you wouldn't. You made that mistake in the past."

He shook his head and for the first time Bianca saw how tired he looked. How run down and sad. The expression on his normally strong face broke her heart.

"You offer me no other choice." He met her eyes and she saw he didn't relish this. "I will not save you from your financial woes until you come home. No matter what troubles befall you."

She broke his gaze. Despite her losses, she had enough money to continue living comfortably in London. She just didn't have many options outside of her current residence. Luckily, she felt no need to travel.

"And what if I don't require saving?" she asked.

His sigh drew her attention back. She'd never heard such defeat in his voice before. "I could have you declared unfit. Not even your husband's will could protect you if the courts determine you need the guardianship of your family."

Bianca stumbled back as the room around her shattered into pieces of color, sound and scent. She had never imagined her own father could make such a devastating threat, but he had. And he meant it. She'd never known him to make an empty promise.

She stared at him in wordless shock and her expression seemed to hurt him as much as his threat had hurt her.

"Don't force me to do that to you, Bianca." Without another glance for her, he walked away. "Don't force me."

Chapter Two

Bianca paced her bedroom. Her thin robe shimmied around her nude body as she pivoted on one heel and stalked back across to the open window to look down onto the street below.

Anger bubbled in her chest, threatened to overflow in a tantrum of childish proportions. How could her father threaten her? Him of all people! He was the very person who had put her in her current state.

Yes, she was aware of the guilt that drove him. He had arranged her marriage and insisted Oscar was the only man she accept. Only after the wedding had they all learned the truth about her husband's appetites. By then, the marriage had been consummated many times over and it was too late for her father to demand her return.

So he had watched as she transformed from an innocent maiden to a sultry woman. She had been forced to take the steps necessary to protect herself from the shocking sensuality that hit her from all sides in Oscar's bed. She had taken control and even grown to enjoy the powerful feelings such erotic decadence awakened in her.

But now Oscar was dead and her family believed she could simply return to the innocence of her life before. She could not. She *would* not return to a life where a man controlled her. Where he could disappoint her like her father had, as Oscar had.

In her current state, *she* controlled her heart. *She* controlled her fate.

At least she had until her father made his devastating threat. He was under the erroneous impression that having her declared unfit and dragging her back home would protect her from herself. With that as his motivation, he wouldn't give her much time to consider his ultimatum and change her lifestyle. A month, perhaps six weeks at most. During that time, she had to find a way to stop him…or escape his reach.

Only escaping was going to be difficult without her full inheritance to finance such a departure. As he had pointed out, a large portion of her inheritance was lining Hawk's pockets thanks to her nights in the hells.

Suppressing a sob, she placed her palm flat against the cool glass. All her dreams and hopes flashed before her eyes and died a terrible death. With Oscar, she had learned she wasn't made for a life of croquet and needlepoint. Or for a 'respectable' husband who would expect her to bow to his will and answer to his rules. She'd developed too much of a taste for the pleasures of life.

The door rattled behind her as Everett slipped into her room with a broad, proprietary smile. Bianca managed to return the expression with a weak version of her own. Though she did like Everett's enthusiasm in bed and his utter devotion to her, at this moment she wasn't in the mood for his touch or his games. She was too caught up in her own troubles. And truth be told, she was beginning to bore of him.

Just as she had bored of every other lover she'd taken since she came out of mourning. No man seemed to satisfy her either physically or intellectually.

"You are so beautiful, love," Everett murmured as he nuzzled his mouth against her throat. "My God, you drove me mad tonight at the Langley party. I wanted nothing more than to take you to one of the bedrooms and have you right there."

Bianca smiled as she reached up to stroke the crisp hair above his collar. Everett wasn't going to be happy when she finally cut ties with him. A man so smitten rarely was, but she would find a way to make the split an amiable one. Her other lovers had accepted their inevitable dismissals and so would this one.

He slipped his hands up to the tie of her robe and slid the knot loose. His fingers were momentarily cold against the smooth skin of her belly and Bianca let out a hiss of sensation. Her nipples puckered as heat from the fireplace brushed over them, then was replaced by the pressure of Everett's thumbs.

She tilted her head back and tried to focus on the feel of him touching her. Despite his other shortcomings, Everett was a skilled lover. He didn't make her heart race, but he knew how to touch her and if she focused hard enough, she always came with his ministrations.

Tonight she needed the sweet oblivion of release.

"Take me to bed, Everett," she sighed as she flicked her tongue out to tease his earlobe. He groaned as he guided her back toward her huge four-poster bed and laid her across the coverlet. "And tell me what you're going to do to me."

His lips curled back. She'd discovered early on that he had a skill at dirty talk. It seemed like the only thing that kept her attention anymore.

"First, I'm going to take this robe off," he said as he yanked the silk down off her shoulders and tossed it into a heap on the floor behind him. "And then I'm going to lick every square inch of your skin. I want to taste you. I want to suck your nipples until you sob with need. I want to make your clit swell with my tongue until your cream overflows. And then…"

She squirmed as he stripped his clothing off. Her body was beginning to ache and her pussy was damp with anticipation. "Then?" she whispered past dry lips.

"I can't wait," he murmured as he traced a finger over the swell of her mound. His fingertip dipped inside and Bianca hissed out frustration. Not only was he teasing her with his touch, but she could also tell by the look in his eyes that his promise to lick her until she begged was an empty one. As had happened more often lately, Everett's ardor overflowed before he could fulfill many of her expectations.

"I want to be inside you Bianca."

He spread her legs wide and lifted her backside with both hands before he positioned his rock-hard cock against her wet slit and thrust forward. Everett let out a long sigh as his eyes fluttered shut.

Bianca closed her own eyes while she slipped her hand down to the place where their bodies met. Spreading her slippery folds aside, she found the hard nub of her clit. As Everett began to grind into her with short, slow thrusts, she let her fingers play, but finding release wasn't easy. She pressed down on the engorged nub, but couldn't find the rhythm she needed to explode.

Above her, Everett grunted as his strokes grew faster and harder. He was going to come soon and if she wanted to find her own pleasure, she would need to relax and focus on sensation, not her worries.

Drawing in a deep breath, Bianca cleared her mind and tried to find a pleasant, erotic place of focus. Immediately, her thoughts turned to Hawk. She had been picturing him more and more while making love in the past few months. As always, his image sent a gush of hot wetness to her pussy. Everett groaned at the increased lubrication and his strokes grew erratic and hard.

Bianca thought of Hawk as he'd been at the party tonight. His scent had been the intoxicating combination of leather and sandalwood, whiskey and maleness. She could easily imagine that mixture wafting over her now in her bed. She pictured Hawk's strong arms wrapped around her as he kissed her with those delectable lips that so often drew her attention when they were bantering during long hours of card play.

Then he would lay her back on her bed and strip his clothing off. His cock would spring free of the confines of his trousers, proud as it jutted toward her in passion, in promise. Even though she'd never seen the thrust of his erection before, Bianca had heard tales of his prowess as a legendary lover.

In her imagination, Hawk spread her legs and then it was him thrusting into her instead of Everett. Her fingers danced wildly over her clit as she lost herself in her fantasy. Her inner muscles spasmed and her legs trembled as the most amazing orgasm she'd had in a long time rolled over her in a wave. It crashed over and over until she gave one final, powerful shudder and flopped back exhausted on the covers with her arm over her eyes.

Everett rolled over beside her, his breath as short and harsh as her own. She realized she'd forgotten about him entirely, but he had obviously experienced his own release. Apparently he hadn't even noticed when she slipped away from him while he fucked her. Thank God she hadn't cried out Hawk's name when she came, or there would be some explaining to do.

She panted as her heart rate slowly dropped back to normal. Hawk was still on her mind. He had her money and she needed that if she wished to flee England and her father's reach. How could she get it back from him?

Everett propped himself up on one elbow and began to trace the lines of her body with a fingertip.

"That was amazing," Everett said softly. "You gripped me so hard. I love to pleasure you like that."

Bianca held back a laugh. Everett had had nothing to do with her pleasure. Hawk had given her that release and he hadn't even needed to be in the room to touch her.

"It was lovely," she reassured him as she pushed off the bed and found her robe. She shoved her arms in and tied it loosely. Her mind still turned over ways to retrieve her money from Hawk without gambling with him. History had proven she couldn't win against him at cards.

Everett stood to wrap his arms around her waist. "Poor darling. You were so distracted by your blasted father tonight. I know he wants you to come back home."

Bianca stiffened and her mind returned from its plotting immediately. How did Everett know that? She hadn't told him and her father and brothers despised him almost as much as they hated Hawk. Her family certainly wouldn't turn to him with their fears and desires. Which meant he had been spying on her.

Her lips thinned as she pulled away from his embrace, but Everett wouldn't let her go so easily.

"Yes," she admitted past a clenched jaw. "He does want me to come home. You may tip your spies well, my dear."

Instead of having the decency to be ashamed, Everett laughed. "I had to know what was causing you such grief." His tone grew serious again. "It is a difficult situation. But I could help you."

She turned to look at him. Everett had less money than she did and she doubted he would let her go if he knew she wished to leave the country. It would mean the end of their affair. "And how could you do that?"

To her shock, he dropped, completely naked, to one knee in the middle of her bedroom. "Marry me, Bianca."

She drew back with a gasp. Her mind went mad with thoughts as she stared down at him. A marriage *could* solve all her problems. Her father would have no right to declare her unfit or remove her from her husband's home.

But she would be legally bound to Everett. Instead of being controlled by her misguided father, she would be under Everett's thumb. That idea wasn't pleasant. Even with no understanding between them, he pressured her to stay away from the hells. And his jealousy had flared more than once when it came to other men, especially her former lovers and Hawk. Even her late husband had been a subject of his never-ending inquisitions and comparisons.

If she took his offer, she would be just as caged as she would be at home. Only she would be trapped with a man she didn't love. And at times, didn't even like.

Given Everett's obvious devotion, she would have to handle this situation delicately. With a gentle smile, she shook her head. "Everett, I do appreciate your offer. I know you're trying to protect me. But I cannot marry you."

Everett stared at her for a long moment and she could see he had never considered she would refuse him. He rose to his feet with stunning quickness and advanced toward her. Even though he was naked and unarmed, Bianca felt a subtle threat in his posture and stepped back in instinctive defense.

"What do you mean you cannot marry me?" he asked. His voice was hoarse and his eyes flashed.

Bianca took another step away and gentled her tone even further. "I'm sorry. I know this hurts you."

"You needn't hurt me," he insisted as he grasped for her hand. His eyes glittered with intensity and a growing anger that concerned Bianca. She didn't let him touch her. His voice went up again. "If you don't wish to hurt me, marry me as I've asked. Why won't you take this offer when it can bring us both so much?"

"Everett, you've been a wonderful lover," she said in an even tone she hoped would calm him. "And I have enjoyed my time with you immensely. But we didn't come together with any thought of marriage. I certainly wouldn't ask you to save me by proposing it."

His face softened and he took her into his arms before she could dodge his ever-seeking grasp another time. "My darling, I knew I wanted to possess you in every way from the first moment I laid eyes on you. It wouldn't be a sacrifice for me to take you as my wife. On the contrary, it would be a wonderful reward."

She struggled to break free of him, but he was surprisingly strong. Bianca sighed. She had tried to be kind, but her attempts to soften the blow only encouraged Everett even more. Now she realized honesty, not flattery, was the only way she would make him see reason.

"Everett, I don't love you," she said firmly. "I could never care for you enough to be your wife. For those reasons, I will not marry you, as much as I appreciate your offer."

At that statement, he did release her so suddenly that Bianca stumbled to the floor. She scrambled to her feet and away from him. His face was dark red with anger. She'd never seen a man turn that color before.

With a curse, he turned away and grabbed for his clothing. He began shoving them on with such violence she was surprised he didn't tear them to shreds. Her heart ached. This was the only part of her affairs she didn't like. Hurting her lover when she was tired of him.

"Everett," she said softly as she reached out to touch his arm in comfort. This time it was he who jerked out of her reach. He spun to face her.

"You bitch," he growled as he buttoned his shirt. "They told me you were nothing but a whore, but I didn't listen."

Bianca drew in a sharp breath of disbelief. "What?"

"You heard me," he snarled. "You're no better than any lightskirt I could pick up off the street, only far more expensive."

"How dare you?" she snapped as the color drained from her face. While she had experienced some loud rows at the end of relationships with other men, none had ever sunk so low as this.

"How dare I?" he roared. "How dare *you*?"

When he moved toward her, she skittered toward the door. If she screamed, her servants might think it was part of her erotic games. Before anyone realized she was in trouble, she could be seriously injured if Everett decided to act on his obviously growing rage.

He grabbed his jacket. "I offered you a chance at respectability again. That is more than any other man will give you, yet you throw it back in my face? As if you were better than I. Well, you'll wish you'd said yes to me sooner than you think."

Bianca set her jaw and threw her door open. "Get out of my house and never come back," she said in a voice that was surprisingly strong considering how angry and frightened she was.

Everett's eyes narrowed, but he did as she said and headed for the door. Before he moved into the hallway and let her close it behind him, he stopped. "You *will* be sorry, Bianca. I promise you that."

She slammed the door behind him and leaned back against it as her breath came in shallow, sharp bursts. She should have expected a man would one day have such a reaction to being rejected, but she'd never thought things could turn so ugly so fast. And never with Everett, who rarely showed an abundance of passion or emotion anywhere but in her bed.

Not that she regretted her choice. Given his startling reaction, she couldn't have born being his wife.

Even if she could have, marriage wasn't the answer to her current woes. Escape was. And only she could arrange for that.

With Hawk's help. She simply had to tap into the desires that already flowed between them. If she did, she could slake her need for him, win her money back and escape her father and Everett, all in one brilliant move.

If only she could get past the wall Hawk always erected between them and reach the part of him that wanted her.

Chapter Three

Hawk strummed his fingers along the arm of a chair in Bianca's sitting room as he tried to fight the swell of excitement that welled inside his chest and his cock. Since Oscar's death two years ago, they had met in gaming hells and ballrooms, but she hadn't invited him into the intimate sanctuary of her residence.

Until today.

His mind spun on the possibilities of what she could want from him. Idle gossip told him her affair with Everett Firth had ended a few days before and ended badly. Since that night, Firth had been holed up with a collection of cheap whores and strong liquor. Hawk hated the bastard, but he almost pitied him. He could only imagine experiencing the bliss of Bianca's body, then losing it. It could drive a man mad, he was sure.

The door opened and Hawk surged to his feet as Bianca entered. Her gown was a benign color, a summer green that highlighted the dark silk of her hair, but the cut of it was bordering on scandalous. It swooped low on her chest, so low that if he slipped his hand beneath the satin he wouldn't have to search very far to find the puckered rigidity of one of her nipples.

The thought hardened him to a painful degree. As Bianca stepped forward, her gaze drifted downward and she smiled in satisfaction at the swell that ballooned his trousers.

"Hawk, thank you so much for accepting my invitation. I know it was abominably short notice. I didn't interrupt anything important, did I?"

She motioned to the settee by the fire. He took a spot on it and was surprised when she joined him, rather than taking a chair across from him. She was being shockingly, delightfully forward and a surge of electric excitement hummed through Hawk's whole body.

"No, nothing at all," he drawled as he watched her pour tea. Even that innocuous activity was made sensual by the way she leaned forward to allow him a generous glimpse of cleavage.

"No afternoon trysts with a woman?" she asked sweetly, as if she had just inquired about the weather.

Hawk swallowed back his surprise and took the cup of tea she offered. "No, Bianca. I'm between mistresses at present and thank you for asking. I hear you're in the same state."

She smiled at his honest answer and gave a laughing one of her own. "Yes, I am on my own again, so it seems. And that is why I've called you here today."

"Yes?" He set the teacup down on its saucer with a clatter and leaned forward. He couldn't mask his anticipation and didn't even bother to try.

"I've come to realize I cannot beat you at cards," she said, before taking a casual sip of her tea.

Hawk wrinkled his brow. It seemed an odd and rather anti-climactic statement to make when sexual tension zinged between them. "Is that so? Does that mean I won't be gaming with you in the hells anymore?"

"I don't know that I'll return to the hells." She tilted her head. "But it doesn't mean I don't wish to gamble with you. You have won a great deal of money from me and I want a chance to take it back."

He was still puzzled, but refused to show her his confusion. Instead he leaned back in the settee and arched an eyebrow. "You intrigue me. If you don't intend to meet me at the tables any longer, how shall you win your money back?"

"With a wager."

He laughed. He never made a bet he couldn't win. Many men had learned that the hard way. "What kind of wager? Horses, cock fights, perhaps a boxing match?"

"No." Now she set her own cup down and leaned closer to him. Her hand dropped casually onto his leg and the implied intimacy of the touch made him jerk in response. She ignored the reaction. "I think it's silly to deny how we're drawn to each other. I will admit I want you, Hawk. I want you more than I've wanted any other man for as long as I can remember. And I think you want me just as much, even though you've kept your distance since Oscar's death."

Hawk's heart was racing so hard, he feared it might burst through his chest before he heard the rest of her offer. And anything that started out so provocatively had to be worthwhile.

"I do want you, Bianca. That has never been a secret," he said and cursed the hoarseness of his voice.

"Then I would like to place a wager based on our mutual…" She laughed. "Attraction to each other." Her hand inched up his knee and she squeezed his thigh lightly. "I want you in my bed for a month, Hawk. I *need* you in my bed for a month."

He grasped the hand she continued sliding higher and higher. He needed to focus. When she was within inches of cupping his erection he couldn't breathe, let alone have coherent thoughts. "And how is that a wager, my dear?"

Her smile twitched bigger. "You and I are similar creatures. We bore of our lovers quickly. But my guess is that you won't tire of *me* in a month. You'll beg me not to leave you when the time comes. And if you do, then I win all my money back."

She slipped her hand away from his and sat back triumphant as she waited for his answer. The answer Hawk couldn't give because he was too busy staring at her in utter amazement. His dream, his fantasy for so many years he'd lost count, had been for Bianca to offer herself to him. Now she had done that… yet it was part of a wager, not for her personal pleasure.

Somehow that stung. Bianca had always been more to him than a mere prize to be won. Apparently she thought less of herself than that.

Less of him.

And he wanted more. So much more.

"I'm not sure," he said.

She blinked, but didn't seem surprised at his lie. "Your cock says differently, Mr. Hawkins. Your mouth and eyes make a good bluff, but your body tells the truth."

Hawk couldn't help but laugh. Bianca had more sparkle than anyone he'd ever known. And she was correct. His body did ache for the chance she offered. It could be his only opportunity with her. And if he could negotiate the terms, perhaps his very best one.

"Let's say I do want to take you up on your offer," he said as he leaned forward to drape his elbows over his knees. His hand brushed her leg as he did so and she hissed out a sigh before she could control the reaction. Hawk smiled. He had proven his point as deftly as she had.

"I knew you would."

"*If* I do, what do I get if *you* fall at *my* feet?"

For the first time since she'd come into the room, Bianca seemed surprised by his answer. Her eyes widened and her face paled as she rose to her feet and paced away. He watched her as she stood with her back to him near the window.

Finally she turned with a shake of her head. "That won't happen."

The absolute assuredness of her tone set Hawk's teeth on edge. And drove him with a desire to prove her wrong. In one smooth motion, he rose to his feet and crossed the distance between them. She opened her mouth to speak, but before she could, he pressed her against the wall and covered her lips with his own.

There was never a moment of resistance. From the second he pinned her with his body, her mouth fell open and Bianca's tongue collided with his. It was a kiss he'd waited years to claim and he savored every moment of it, memorizing the fresh taste of her and the way her tongue tangled with his. She had as much aggression as he, taking as much as he gave, and clinging to his shoulders with both hands until he actually felt her nails cutting through his shirt.

He clawed for her breast and cupped it, then dipped his hand beneath the neckline as he'd imagined doing when she entered the room. Her nipple swelled and hardened against his fingers and she let out a harsh cry of pleasure that was lost in his mouth. She arched against him and their pelvises collided. The friction was painful bliss and Hawk wanted so much more.

But he wouldn't take it yet. Not until he had an answer to his question.

Deftly, he slid his fingers out of her dress and stepped back. He steadied her with one hand and smiled when she stared up at him in desire.

"What? Why did you stop?" she asked in utter shock. Apparently, this was a new experience for her.

He tilted his head. "Like you, I was proving a point. You say you won't beg, but I think I've shown you that it could and will happen."

Her swollen lips thinned to a frown and her blue eyes narrowed to slits. "You don't know what you're talking about."

He cupped her breasts and nudged the hard bead of her nipple that thrust against the silk. Bianca's head dipped back as she gasped.

"Your body can't bluff, either, Bianca," he whispered before he released her. "So if you end up begging me for more after our month together, what will *I* receive?"

She shrugged, but her wide eyes told him how much she was affected by him. "You can keep the money."

He laughed. "Not good enough. You're giving me something I already have."

"I-I-" she stammered.

Hawk flushed in triumph. He'd never seen Bianca so off balance before. And he had done that to her. With a kiss and a refusal to let her lead this game she wanted him to play. By taking the upper hand, he'd stymied her entirely.

"Max," she blurted out. "You can have Max."

"Oscar's horse?"

She nodded swiftly. "You've always coveted him."

Hawk shook off his surprise. "Yes. I did, but I don't want him now."

She looked like she wanted to stomp her foot in frustration. "What then?"

He looked her up and down and his body clenched with need. This could be his only chance to tell her the truth. A risk he had to take if he wanted her. And oh, how he wanted her. Even more now that he'd had a taste.

"You. I have always coveted you. More than any amount of money. More than any horse. I won't beg for you, Bianca. If at the end of a month, you want to leave, I shall let you go without an argument. But I do want you."

She groped behind her for the back of a chair and leaned on it with all her weight. She was so pale Hawk thought she might faint.

"What?" The word barely carried.

"You know, Bianca." He stepped forward. "You've always known or you wouldn't have come to me with this offer. If I enter into this wager with you and at the end of the month you're begging me for more, then I want you. For as long as I want you, however I want you. As my mistress."

* * *

Bianca reeled back until her rear end hit the wall next to the window Hawk had pressed her against not moments before. His mistress? God, the possibilities that one little word created! His bed. His life. By his side. Forever.

Or at least until he bored of her and found someone else.

Her heart dropped at that thought. Her time with Oscar had taught her how much power she could wield with her body. But she was no fool. Desire could be used against her, as well.

That was why she had always been the one to throw over the lovers in her life. She'd never been the one to be sent on her way.

Hawk wasn't like the other men who had shared her bed. If she stayed with him for more than a month, she wouldn't ever want to leave. And she couldn't bear his rejection when he was through with her.

Even if she could, becoming his lover wouldn't solve her problem. In fact, it would compound it. Her father wouldn't stand for the hated Lucius Hawkins taking her as a mistress. He would definitely have her declared unfit if that happened and even Hawk couldn't protect her from the consequences of that action. She couldn't have it.

So she was back to her original plan. Take Hawk to her bed for one month, but keep him from her heart. Give him all her body, but none of her soul. If she could do that, she knew he wouldn't want to let her go. He was a man after all, driven by baser needs. If she could manage to stay aloof, he would be as easy to tame as every other man who'd spent time in her bed.

"Very well." She forced a slow, sultry smile, then moved toward him. "Have we agreed to the terms of the wager then? Do you accept my bet?"

Hawk shook his head. "Not quite yet. I have one more question."

She froze. Why wouldn't he simply acquiesce? No other man had ever given her so much trouble! She couldn't control the peevish tone to her voice. "Yes?"

"Why are you doing this now, Bianca?" He folded his arms. "What makes you need your money back so desperately?"

She shivered. If she told Hawk the truth, she put herself at a distinct disadvantage. He would be privy to her troubles and her desperation to escape her father's threats.

If she had learned anything from facing him across a card table, it was to never give Hawk the upper hand.

"Who says this bargain is about money?" She took his hand and slowly lifted it to her cheek. She was pleased when his eyes fluttered shut for just a moment. He had a weakness, too, and she intended to exploit it. "Perhaps I've simply decided our time has come and the money only makes it more dangerous. More interesting. Now stop toying with me, Hawk. I won't ask again. Do you or do you not take me up on this wager?"

His fingers curled on her cheek as his other hand swiftly encircled her waist. "With pleasure, my lady," he growled before his mouth came down on hers.

As it had been the first time they kissed, Bianca melted. His touch was like fire and she longed to burn. They fell back onto the settee with his body pressing hers into the cushions. She was trapped, in more ways than one. Not only did his weight not allow her to control the pace of their physical interaction, but his touch pulled away her control over her own reactions.

A spike of self-doubt flashed through her. If he could do this with a simple kiss, what would happen when he took her? When he made her cry out with absolute pleasure?

The images sent a hot gush of wet desire through her body and made her moan against his skillful lips.

No! She had to maintain control. Her very life was at stake. If she was going to make him come to heel, make him beg for her after a month of pleasure, she would need the focus and power her body had possessed for so long. She couldn't give that over to him and win.

With a low growl, she speared her tongue between his lips, but he countered by gently sucking it. Her eyes rolled back of their own accord. The gentle pulling went straight through her body, tightening her nipples painfully against her silken gown and sending a flood of need to dampen her thighs. For the first time in a long time, she truly needed a man. Not just any man, this man. She wanted him to rip her clothing to shreds. She wanted him to wrap her legs around his waist. To bury himself as deeply as he would go. She wanted to lay helpless beneath him while he did it and just enjoy the pleasures of his skilled hands and tongue and cock.

Despite the fact that surrender was her path to ruination.

Hawk gripped the hem of her skirt and pushed it up. Bianca smiled. Here was where she would wrest control from him. She wore nothing beneath her thin gown. Once he discovered that fact, he would be panting and wouldn't be able to keep himself from having her right then and there. Where he lost control, she would sweep it up and wield it over him.

But he didn't act surprised at the discovery. He actually laughed as his hands glided up her bare, smooth legs and his fingers found the slick, hot entrance to her sex. He teased her mercilessly, tracing her slit, but never touching her clit or delving deeply inside her. She tried to remain still, to keep kissing him as if his torture didn't bother her, but finally she arched up with a groan.

"Begging already?" he whispered as he cruelly removed his hand and pushed her skirt back down. "You told me you were better at this than cards."

She pushed against his chest with all her might until she was able to put a little space between them. Dragging her nails down the front of his shirt, she reached for the buttons of his fly. She'd show him torture when she had his cock in her hand.

Hawk laughed, a low and seductive sound that made her clit tingle and her nipples grow even more sensitive to the rasping glide of her gown. He caught her hand before she could touch the first button of his fly and pushed it away.

She reached for him again, but he dodged her as he suddenly stood up, leaving her sprawled across her couch like a wanton.

"Why are you stopping?" she panted as she watched him casually straighten his cravat and smooth his tangled hair back into place.

"I have waited for this moment for years, Bianca," he said and at least she was rewarded with the fact that his voice shook. "Too long to make your sitting room the first place where I take you."

She scrambled off the settee so quickly that she stumbled. "What?"

How could this be happening? She had felt his cock pressing against her like velvet steel. She still saw it jutting toward her. Yet he stopped? No man stopped! No man had ever gone as far as Hawk had, then left her wet and wanting.

He smiled. A wicked smile that told her how easily he read her thoughts. "Tonight. Come to my town home after midnight and we'll begin your wager."

Bianca's mouth fell open. Midnight was hours away. She was so full of desire her knees were actually shaking and she was sure her gown was soaked where it had brushed her thighs. How could she wait so long for release?

"Do you agree?" he asked before he reached forward and pushed her jaw shut with one finger.

She yanked away from his hand and tried to appear as if she didn't care that he'd left her in such a state.

"Fine. After midnight," she ground out through clenched teeth.

"Until then."

Without so much as a kiss goodbye, Hawk turned and left her sitting room. He even shut the door behind him.

Bianca sank back into the settee. When her dress brushed the heated flesh at the juncture of her thighs, she groaned. Damn the man. He had left her with a powerful reminder of how much control he already wielded over her. That he could leave her so wet and wanting that by the time she reached him that night she would be begging for his touch.

"Oh, no I won't," she muttered as she lay back against the pillows. The servants had been given express instructions not to bother her while she was in this room, so she felt no worry when she glided her skirts up to her hips.

She slid her hand down and touched the puffy nether lips of her pussy. They were sopping wet with her juices and she ached when she brushed along them to find her clit.

She moaned as she slid a finger inside herself while she used her other hand to bear down on the tender nub of flesh. She pictured Hawk and her hips bucked up. He had hardly touched her at all really, but she was affected this powerfully. And tonight she would have more.

Sweating, she stroked her fingers inside and along her clit. Her hips twisted, her breath came short as she built toward a blazing release. Already the inner walls of her womb contracted madly until she gripped her own finger like a vice and a wet gush of cream coated her hand. She trembled and cried out with the power of her pleasure.

For a long time, she simply laid on the settee, too exhausted by her orgasm to move. When she withdrew her fingers, her pussy immediately began to ache again. She let out a low curse. It seemed she could pleasure herself all day, but what her body truly craved was Hawk.

Whatever else happened, he could not be allowed to stroke her to such a fever pitch again.

Rising to her feet, she smoothed her skirts and paced to the window. "I will break Hawk," she muttered to her wavy reflection in the glass. "And I shall start tonight."

Chapter Four

Hawk rested his forehead against his front door. He could actually *feel* Bianca's heat as she stood on the stoop waiting to be allowed in. His cock readied at the knowledge that she was there. There for him.

He lifted his head. No matter what happened, no matter what she did, he had to remember his strategy. Bianca needed mastery. She too often got her way in life and in love. She used her body as a tool for control. If he was going to win her wager, win her, he'd have to take that control, no matter what manner of sensual trickery she launched at him.

Drawing a deep breath, he opened the door.

For a moment, his thoughts of mastery and control fluttered away as he stared at her. In the circle of light coming from the doorway, she looked like a fallen angel in her white satin gown. Lace covered the shockingly low neckline, but beneath the fabric he saw skin. The little yellow flowers that had been painstakingly embroidered in a fall along the front of her skirt implied innocence, but the sultry look in her eyes said sin.

And then there was her scent. Vanilla and rainwater. Heather and lust. The same combination that had been driving him wild for years. Tonight he would immerse himself in it, surround himself with her. And he couldn't wait.

"I've miscalculated your station, Mr. Hawkins, if you must open your own door," she said with a saucy wink, but her voice was husky and strained. "Must I stand out on your stoop all night?"

With a start, Hawk stepped back to allow her entry. As she passed by him in a cloud of heat and intoxicating scent, he did his best to collect himself.

Mastery. Control.

Grabbing her arm, he spun her around and used their combined weights to slam the door shut. He pressed her back, tilting his hips to rub his aching body against her. She let out a quiet moan while she tilted her face and fluttered her eyes shut.

Hawk smiled. She wanted a kiss. As much as he wanted to give her that, he refused. Instead, he shoved his fingers into the silky web of her hair and glided each and every pin free to clatter on the foyer floor. Waves of silky hair tumbled around him, catching him in a web of heat. He caught a blue-black lock and raised it to his nose for a long whiff. The scent made him weak, but her frustrated groan made him strong.

"I only open my own door when I have dismissed my servants for the night." He paused for full effect. "All night."

To his delight, Bianca shivered in reaction and the pulse that throbbed at the base of her throat increased its rate two fold.

"Did you?" Her voice wavered.

He nodded as he rubbed his rough cheek against her satin one. Her husky sigh reverberated in his ear and set his blood on fire. "I like the idea of being able to take you anywhere." To accentuate that statement, he surged against her with his pelvis. "To possess you in any way I please without any possibility of interruption."

"Oh, God."

Her little whispered plea and the way she stared up at him with clouded, need-filled eyes made Hawk's erection jolt of its own accord. He dipped his head and finally took the kiss he'd been denying them both. Her mouth fell open and he thrust inside, swirling and tasting until his body shook with dizzying need.

Control.

With effort, he pulled back. Winning this bet was very important. It seemed more important than taking his next breath at the moment. Even before he had her the first time, he knew a month with Bianca wouldn't be nearly enough to slake what he had desired for so long.

"Come with me," he said as he took a painful step away from her and offered her his hand. After being in such close quarters, pulling back felt like having an ice bath, but it was necessary. His goal tonight was to make her plead with him. The only way to insure that was to deny her whatever she desired most.

Even if it meant denying himself in the process.

Bianca followed him up the stairs in uncharacteristic silence and didn't protest when they entered his bedchamber. She didn't look around, even though she'd never been upstairs in his home before. She didn't even seem to notice the huge bed that had been made up with sinful satin sheets.

She stared only at him. Her hunger was plain, unhidden and she wasn't embarrassed by it. That direct, pure desire was intriguing, powerful… And Hawk wanted it all.

Still, when she stepped forward and tried to wrap her arms around his neck, he caught her hands and pinned them behind her back. She squirmed for a moment, then stopped. Her blue eyes came back up to his face, but there was no hint of pleading in them yet.

She rose up on her tiptoes and lifted her mouth to his. He dodged her kiss even though his lips ached. Now her eyes flew open.

"Hawk!" she protested softly.

He didn't answer, but pushed her back until she fell onto the bed. Using one hand, he lifted her arms over her head and held down them against the satin. He restrained her legs by throwing one of his own over both of hers. To his surprise, Bianca didn't struggle. Instead, she looked up at him with a smooth, hot smile.

"I see," she whispered. "I see what you like."

Her voice made his ears tingle and his erection lengthen. He cursed himself for being so aroused by her. There was no doubt she knew it and would use that as her weapon of choice. Not that he blamed her. She certainly couldn't fight him physically, but she could toy with him using her sultry words and the needful expression on her face.

His only defense was to go on the attack. Still holding her arms over her head, he dragged the buttons on the front of her gown open to the waist. Shoving the silk and lace aside, he grasped the thin layer of her chemise and yanked. It tore easily, baring her from the waist up.

Hawk gasped. He had imagined Bianca in this state for so long, but he'd never pictured her to be so beautiful. Her breasts were the perfect size to fill his hands, with rosy nipples and a darker areola that puckered as he looked at her. Using his free hand, he traced the edge of the dusky flesh, reveling in her soft sigh and the way she arched up just a little to force him to increase his touch.

Even though he should have resisted her silent order, he couldn't help himself. He *wanted* to touch her, to cup her breast and turn her sigh into a moan. His free hand curled around one globe, gently kneading the soft flesh until he palmed one hard nipple.

He glanced up. Bianca was biting her lower lip with enough force that he was surprised she didn't draw blood. With a smile, he realized she was trying not to cry out. His game was working and now it was time to make it even more difficult for her to resist.

Dipping his head, he let jut the tip if his tongue dart out to sweep across the tight nub of flesh. He swirled it around the edge of her nipple, sampling the sweet wine of her skin in little darts and laps. Bianca's breathing increased, but she still didn't cry out. He couldn't help but admire her control, even though he was more determined than ever to break it.

Hawk let his licks become firmer and last longer as he toyed with her nipple until it shone in the candlelight, jutting out in proud announcement of her desire. Finally, when her breath was coming in sharp, deep gasps, he sucked her between his lips.

Her cry was like music to his ears. A long, harsh wail that seemed to echo in the silent room and filled him with triumph. His blood rushed as her hips tilted up, knocking her thighs against his cock in a delicious, tortuous fashion.

"Tell me you need me," he ordered as he started a hot trail from one breast to another. "Beg me."

She shook her head, though it was clear the motion took considerable effort. "No."

With a laugh, he started his torture over again, this time on her opposite breast. Again, she writhed; working doubly hard to hold back her gasps and cries, but failing the moment he took her nipple between his lips and suckled.

He released her with reluctance and pulled her to a sitting position. Now that he wasn't holding her arms down, she immediately grasped his shoulders. Her fingers kneaded into the muscles there, her fingernails grazed his skin and sent sensation throbbing through him.

"Stop," he ordered as he backed away from the bed.

Her eyes cleared slightly and she looked up at him in hurt confusion and wild desperation. "Why? Don't tell me you're going to leave me like you did earlier."

He smiled. So his trick had worked. Leaving her needy had given him power, power he would require if he wanted to take this wager at the end. "If you try to touch me when I haven't given you leave to do so, I will desert you as I did this afternoon."

She clenched her fists. "I want to touch you."

He grabbed her skirt at the hips and pulled until it yanked free. Her shredded chemise went just as quickly, then her boots and stockings. In as much time as it took her to draw her next breath of protest, he stripped her naked.

"That's unfortunate," he murmured. "I suppose you'll have to learn to live with disappointment."

She clenched her jaw, her eyes following him as he shucked off his own clothing. He tracked her gaze to his cock. It jutted upward in a carnal display of his desire. He was pleased when she wet her lips, though it put a painful image of her suckling him into his mind.

"You know," she purred as she lay back on the bed. She spread her long legs to give him a view meant to entice. "I could simply pleasure myself as I did after you left me this afternoon."

Hawk barely held back a moan. How he would love to see her strum herself to an orgasm. To see her fingers tangle in the wet warmth of her pussy, arch up beneath her own touch.

She smiled wickedly, fully aware of what her casual comment did to him. "If you won't let me have what I want, I don't really need you."

"Don't you?" He arched a brow before he gripped his cock in his right hand and stroked it from base to tip in one smooth action. Pleasure shot through him but he knew it was nothing when compared to what he'd find when he entered her. Still, he had to bluff.

The bluff paid off when she squealed, "No, wait!"

She sat up with difficulty as the sheets slithered beneath her shapely backside. "Very well. Tonight I'll do as you ask." Her eyes narrowed in warning. "But don't think you've won me yet."

Hawk didn't try to mask his triumph. "Lay back."

In a last show of defiance, she followed his order as slowly as she could. But when she settled her head on his pillows, he saw she had truly surrendered to his will. It was a first step. The next was to make her ask for what she wanted. Beg.

He crawled up the bed, nudging her legs apart to lie between them. He could already smell the dark musk of her sex, calling to him, asking him to fill her. His own body responded, but he held back. It wasn't time to have her yet. Not until she needed it above anything else. Not until she sobbed with desire.

He kissed the smooth curve of her belly, rubbed the rough stubble of his cheek against her skin. Her hands stirred at her sides, but she gripped them into fists with a purse of her lips.

With light nips and nibbles, Hawk feasted on her, tasting the swell of her hip, the curve of her outer thigh. She gasped when he crooked her knee and suckled the inside and he made a mental note of it. He needed to know every single pleasure point, every weakness if he was going to make her crave him more than breathing, more than life.

She thrust her hips up, saying without words where she wanted his lips and tongue. Normally, Hawk would have fulfilled her request, but tonight he needed her desires to be spoken. Instead of moving toward her core, he teased her thighs.

Hawk glided his hands beneath Bianca's backside, lifting her up in offering and spreading her sex as a result.

Her breathing increased, but he still didn't touch her where her desire was flowing like wine and her flesh was quivering. He looked at her, spread open to him in utter acquiescence. Her pussy was as beautiful as the rest of her. Dark with desire, shining with need.

Bianca let out a low, pained moan. It wasn't the words Hawk wanted, but it was good enough that he let his hand cup her. She sighed with relief and shivered. Her outer lips clenched at him, trying to pull him in, trying to find that touch that would release her from the sweet agony she was experiencing.

Hawk drew in deep breaths. It took all his concentration to block out the intense throb of his erection as he fingered her. He spread her with his thumb and forefinger, just rimming the opening to a place better than heaven, then dipped inside. She clenched around him with a cry, pulsing on the edge of an orgasm he was determined to deny her.

Slipping a second digit inside her tight sheath, Hawk bent his head forward and lightly licked her clit. Her wail turned into a scream, a cry of frustration and relief merged into one. Her earthly flavors filled his senses as he went to work in earnest on her clit. When she shivered close to release, he removed his lips, but continued to flex his fingers inside her.

"If you tell me what you want, I'll give it to you," he promised as he blew a gust of hot breath on her swollen sex. "You just have to say please."

She glared down at him as she continued to writhe in blissful agony. "You know what I want," she panted, her tone strangled by continued efforts to remain in control.

"I apologize, but that isn't the proper answer," he teased before allowing another light lick. One that was meant to make her throb, not give release.

Her guttural moan rocked through him. With a sob, she said, "Suck me, Hawk. Lick me. Make me come with your mouth. Now."

He'd ordered her to say please, but her command was a good enough start. Delving down, he caught her clit between his lips and suckled. She ground against him with a cry, thrusting in time to his tongue-lashing until finally he felt her shiver and quake before a massive release.

But instead of allowing her pleasure, he removed his fingers and slid up her body. He pinned each arm with one hand until he had caged her in his embrace.

"Do you want release?" he whispered close to her lips.

"Yes, God yes!" she screamed as she thrust her hips up.

"Then say please."

Her gaze met his with such heat he almost turned away from its intensity. "Please Hawk! Please!"

"Thank God," he moaned as he spread her legs wide and impaled her in one smooth motion. Her sex contracted wildly around him as she put her mouth against his shoulder and screamed out the most powerful release he'd ever felt a woman experience. She thrashed against his thrusts, taking every hard glide with a turn of her hips and a squeeze of her internal muscles.

His cock swelled and his balls tightened in painful, magical bliss as he neared his own release. He wanted her to quiver around him, to make her cry out one last time before he spilled his seed. He released one of her hands and dipped his fingers between them. Finding her clit, he ground down on her.

She arched up again, tears streaming down her face as she gripped at the sheets and trembled around him. Hawk thrust deep, deeper. Deep enough he feared he might be lost.

Or perhaps found.

And then the world shattered around him as he filled her with his essence amidst an earth-shaking cry he realized came from his own lips. Her cry merged with his until the room echoed and shook.

In a few moments, Hawk realized he was breathing again. His vision was no longer blurred and shaking. And Bianca was staring up at him with eyes that were totally unreadable. And beautiful in the dying candlelight.

He collapsed onto her sweat slick body with a final moan and wrapped his arms around her while his mind cried out in triumph.

Finally, he had claimed Bianca's body. Now to lay claim on the rest of her.

Chapter Five

Bianca groaned as another delicious ache crested through her body. She sank lower into the steaming bathwater and stared at the ceiling with a satisfied smile. The achy muscles were well-worth it. Her first night with Hawk had gone well beyond all her fantasies.

Quite a feat considering she'd been dreaming of him for so many years. Even before Oscar's death, Hawk's face and body had haunted her private thoughts.

Her only complaint about their night together was that she hadn't been able to touch him, please him, as he had pleased her. It was a significant change from her other lovers. Normally, she took the lead. Even when a man claimed her, she was the driving force behind every stroke, every burst of pleasure.

Not with Hawk. He had controlled her. Melted her. Made her cry with frustration as much as she had sobbed with pleasure when he finally gave her release after release.

She'd all but forgotten how good that felt.

She smiled at the memory and enjoyed the shiver that rocked her body, despite the hot bath water. Her eyes fluttered shut and she relived every sinful moment of the night before.

Hawk pressing her against his door, not able to wait to get upstairs. Hawk pinning her arms behind her back.

Above her head. Stripping her and demanding she surrender to him.

A gasp escaped her lips as her eyes flew open. Surrender. Hawk may have made it seem like he was out of control with lust, but in the end, it was *she* who had surrendered with very little fight. She'd pleaded with him to enter her, to make her come.

"It was a trap," she murmured to herself as she covered her mouth with her wet hand. "A way to whittle away my resistance, piece by piece."

She slammed a hand against the water's surface, sending a splash over the edge to slap the floor below. How could she have been so foolish? She had let her baser needs rule her mind and Hawk had taken the upper hand in their wager for the second time!

The pleasure of memory fled, replaced by sobering thoughts about the seriousness of her situation. To win this wager... to keep her heart, she could not give Hawk what had been taken last night.

Folding her arms, she leaned back. "Not again. Tonight will be different. Tonight I will insure you come to heel beneath *me*."

The thought conjured a lovely image. One of Hawk sprawled out on that sinful bed of his. Her straddling him, teasing him with her lips, with the sweep of her hair, with deft fingers. Then, when he was writhing beneath her, she would drop her slick heat over his erection and ride him until he was blind with need and couldn't help but come deep within her.

She sighed as she let her fingers play over her breast in the warm water. That would be delicious.

Just as she was about to let herself find pleasure in the fantasy, a loud commotion erupted in the hallway.

"No, sir! Her ladyship is not at home!"

She frowned. Her butler's voice and a few screams from her maids were compounding the racket. She rose out of the bathwater just as the door to her chamber flew open. It bounced off her wall with a crash to reveal Everett Firth.

"My God," she cried as she grasped for a towel to cover herself.

His eyes grew wide at the sight of her standing naked in her tub, droplets of water shimmying down her in a waterfall. Even when she wrapped a towel around herself, she could tell by his expression that he had burned the image in his mind and was imagining her in all her glory.

Three footmen and her elderly butler, Carson burst into the room behind Everett. The men gasped and several averted their eyes when they saw her nudity. Behind the group, she heard feminine shrieks. The maids, no doubt.

Stepping out of the tub, Bianca did her best to straighten her shoulders and look regal. There was no use making the situation worse than it already was.

"I don't remember inviting you today, Everett," she said and was pleased her voice sounded cool and calm even though this unexpected situation both terrified and humiliated her. "Is there some reason why you couldn't send a card like a normal gentleman caller?"

Everett's face darkened to the same startling red it had when she refused his proposal. Despite her attempts to look composed, she couldn't help stepping away. Even with all the men at her door holding him back, Everett's rage sent icy fear through her.

"You spent the night with *him*," he hissed as he clenched and unclenched his fists.

For the first time in years, Bianca actually blushed. She had no illusions her servants knew about her scandalous antics. Hell, they probably even talked about them. But that didn't mean she wanted to have a discussion about whom she fucked in front of a group of at least ten between the men at her door and the maids who were still tittering in the hall.

She folded her arms across her breasts. "I beg your pardon."

"With Hawkins." He pulled against the footmen's hold, but they strained to keep him back. "I know you spent the night in his bed."

With difficulty, Bianca managed to keep her surprise from her face. How could Everett know that? She had been very discreet and she knew Hawk well enough to know he wouldn't discuss their relationship until the wager had been won. Which meant Everett continued to spy on her.

"Release Mr. Firth, if you please," she said softly.

Carson looked at her with concern. "My lady, he's wild. He could-"

She smiled at the old man. "I understand, Carson. But Mr. Firth is a gentleman. I'm sure he wouldn't do anything he would come to regret later."

Her reminder of his station did exactly what she'd hoped. It tamed the beast in Everett's eyes and he relaxed. Carefully, the footmen released him, though not a one moved to give the two former lovers privacy. A fact Bianca was grateful for despite her lingering embarrassment.

"You spent the night with him, didn't you?" he repeated. This time his voice was low.

She pursed her lips. "You and I are no longer affiliated, Everett. You should find another lover. I'm sure with your skills-"

She blushed again as her butler jerked his face away. This really wasn't a conversation she wished to have in front of servants, but there was nothing to be done about it. Everett had snatched control from her with his intrusion.

Straightening her spine, she continued, "With your skills in the bedroom, any lady would be pleased to have you. Once you find someone new, I'm sure you will forget all about me."

Everett's eyes narrowed. "Did you spend a night with Lucius Hawkins?" he repeated slowly and loudly.

Bianca's anger bubbled up in her chest. How dare this man violate her home and talk about her life in front of a crowd?

"I did. And it was wonderful. What of it?" she snapped.

Before she or her protective servants could react, Everett lunged across the room. He caught her bare arm to prevent her escape then slapped her with the back of his free hand. He hit her so hard that stars danced before her eyes and pain shot from her cheek down to her teeth and up to her ear.

He was yanked away before he could do worse. She stumbled when the footmen wrenched his hands from her arms, but managed to right herself.

"How could you?" Everett wailed as they dragged him away. "You are mine until I say otherwise. I won't have you sharing yourself with any other man."

"I'm sorry, so sorry," Carson said as the footmen dragged Everett out of her room and down the hall. With a bow, he allowed her personal maid into the room, then shut the door behind himself.

Once he was gone, Bianca sank to her knees in a shaking heap. Her maid rushed to her side.

"Oh, my lady!" the girl gasped through her own tears.

Bianca pulled the towel around herself even tighter as she got to her feet. She clung to the girl as she led her to the bed. "It's alright, Emmaline. Please don't cry. I'm not hurt and Mr. Firth is gone," she gasped when she was able to speak. "Get me my robe."

The sobbing maid nodded blindly and fetched her dressing gown from the chair beside the bed. As Bianca pulled it on, she noticed Everett had left light, finger-shaped bruises on her arm. She wouldn't doubt her face would be the same in a few hours. What Hawk would do about that made her shiver.

"We tried to stop him, ma'am," Emmaline said as she took a crumpled handkerchief from her apron pocket.

"I know you did."

Bianca forced a wavering smile to comfort the other woman. What she really wanted to do was sink back on her bed and have a cry of her own, but she'd already made enough of a spectacle of herself in front of her staff for one day.

"He was mad!" the maid sighed.

Bianca dipped her head. She, too, had seen madness in Everett's eyes. It was nothing she had experienced. She'd had lovers who became possessive in the past, yes. But it had never been like this. None had ever been so bold as to attack her in her own home. Most had just sent flowers and tried to change her mind in ballrooms until her gentle refusals finally sunk in.

Glancing up, she saw Emmaline was still staring at her with round, red-rimmed eyes. Bianca drew a breath and put on her best 'mistress of the house' smile.

"He's gone now though, isn't he? I'm sure Carson and the other men will be on a lookout for him in the future and he won't dare to return after the awful scene he made. If he does, I shall authorize Carson to shoot him on sight."

At that, Emmaline giggled and Bianca relaxed a little. The last thing she wanted was for her staff to live in terror. Hopefully the way she dismissed the incident would calm everyone once word circulated below stairs.

If only she could calm herself so easily.

"I will be out for the evening again tonight," she said, rising as if she'd already forgotten the entire scene. "I will need the red gown. Get my things ready, I'll be dressing in an hour."

With a brisk curtsey, Emmaline left the room to make arrangements. Once she'd gone, Bianca crumpled back onto her bed and curled up on her side with her arms around her pillow. She shivered, not just because of what Everett had done, but because while he had been terrorizing her, she had thought of Hawk and wished he'd been there to save her.

And wishing on a man like Hawk was dangerous.

Wager Of Sin

* * *

"My God, you do look delectable," Hawk said as he came into the sitting room where Bianca had been told to wait. She'd been disappointed to discover his servants were home this night, but now her frustration fled as Hawk's eyes sparked with passion.

For a moment, she forgot the game and crossed the room, drawn by a desire to be near him. To touch him. She stopped a few inches in front of him to look up into his gray eyes. After her trying afternoon, she merely wanted his strength for just an instant before she forced herself back into the wager she had made.

When she rested her cheek against his shoulder and simply clung to him, Hawk seemed surprised. Then his arms came around her and his fingers slowly traced a soothing pattern on her back.

With a sigh, she stepped away, determined to put all her concentration into their wager tonight and win her first battle in their sensual war. When she smiled, he didn't return the expression.

"What is it?" he asked as he quietly shut the door to give them privacy.

She blushed, a terrible habit she hadn't seemed to be able to shake since she made the wager with Hawk. With a start, she turned away from his all-seeing stare.

"I was just… eh, happy to see you," she lied.

He touched her arm and gently guided her back to face him. "No, that isn't it. Something has happened."

Bianca sank her teeth into her lower lip. Never had she thought Hawk would see her emotions so clearly. A part of her was exhilarated by the thought that he could see her soul with just a glance. Another part was shaken. How was she to win her money back if he could see her tiniest upset and read her deepest, hidden pains? He was too close and she had vowed long ago never to let a man close to her heart.

"It's silly, really." She laughed as if her troubles were nothing at all. "Apparently news of our first night together has gotten out into society, despite my best efforts to keep it private. Someone told me they knew my secret today."

Her breath caught in her throat as she tried not to focus on that afternoon in her bedchamber and the fears that had nothing to do with their wager being discovered.

Hawk laughed as he crossed over to the bar and fixed them each a sherry. "Is that all? I wouldn't think that would matter to you much."

With a forced smile, she turned toward him. "No, I suppose it was only a matter of time before the news got out. And we never said we'd keep our relationship a sec-"

"What happened to your cheek?" Hawk's voice was suddenly icy as he set both drinks on the poor boy and stalked across the room toward her.

Bianca froze. She and Emmaline had tried very hard to cover the light bruise on her face, but Hawk cupped her chin and tilted her face so he could see the mark. His lips thinned and a fire lit in his eyes that made Bianca want to back away. Not because she was afraid for her own safety as she had been that afternoon, but because she knew she couldn't stop the storm that would blow in the wake of his anger.

"It isn't anything, Hawk," she whispered as she tried to turn away.

He caught her shoulders. "Don't lie to me. What really happened?"

Looking up into his stormy gray eyes, Bianca's weakness took over. Tears pricked her, the ones she had been unable to shed over her fright that day. Now she struggled to keep them at bay. Hawk wasn't her partner or her friend. He was her adversary and to show him weakness or that she needed him, gave him the upper hand.

"Bianca," he whispered and his voice had gentled. "Please. Forget the game for a moment."

His warm breath caressed her skin and her eyes fluttered shut as she regulated her own breathing. She could lie all she wanted, but eventually Hawk would find out the truth. It seemed best just to confess now and deal with his reaction immediately.

"It seems my last lover is not at all pleased that I have taken up a new relationship so quickly after ending our affiliation."

Hawk's grip on her shoulders loosened. "Everett Firth did this to you?" he said in a harsh, low voice that cut through Bianca. She'd never heard the usually playful Hawk sound like that.

She met his eyes. "It was nothing. He has spent his anger now and I'm sure he won't be fool enough to do such a thing again. My servants will keep him away."

"And why were they unable to keep him away today?" he snapped as he stormed over to the poor boy and downed his forgotten drink in one gulp.

She shifted in her spot. "He pushed past them."

His glare darted over to her. "I see. And yet you believe they will be able to protect you if he chooses to return and take out his jealousy and betrayal on you again?"

With a purse of her lips, Bianca turned to the fire, away from his knowing stare. He was only voicing her own fears, the ones that had been nagging at her for hours. That Everett would come back and do more than just call her names and slap her. They were terrifying thoughts she didn't want to face.

"My God, this *is* the first time he did such a thing, isn't it?"

Bianca gasped. "Of course! I wouldn't be fool enough to stay with a man who struck me. Today was the first time and in the future I'm sure my servants will be more aware of his potential for violence."

She heard him slam the empty glass down on the table. "Until our wager is over, or at least until Firth can be dealt with, you will stay in my home."

Bianca's mouth dropped open as she spun to face him. He was staring at her with arms folded, his eyes daring her to refuse his command. She folded her own and gave him just as cool and steely a glare.

"I think not. I'm comfortable in my home."

"It's not your comfort I'm worried about," he said quietly. "It's your safety. Perhaps your very life."

That comment sent a shiver through Bianca, but she managed to keep her outward appearance calm. "This is ridiculous," she insisted.

He clenched a fist and worked at regulating his ragged breathing. "Do you truly think so little of yourself?"

She shook her head. "I don't take your meaning."

"You are so determined to keep your precious control that you would endanger your life?" He pursed his lips and beneath the frustration and anger she saw something in his expression that turned her stomach and brought hot blood to her cheeks.

Pity.

"You go too far," she whispered as she struggled with her emotions.

"No, not nearly far enough," he countered. "You have been alone so long you have forgotten what it is to have the protection of someone who cares for you."

She drew in a harsh breath as pain and joy exploded in her heart at once. Hawk cared for her? No, she didn't want that! "Stop."

He ignored her request. "You have forgotten what it is like to trust another person with your troubles."

Tears pricked behind her eyes and she blinked furiously to keep them at bay.

He stopped speaking those wonderful and terrible words and his stare grew more focused. "Or have you ever experienced that at all?"

He was too close. To the truth. To the past. To her heart. With a cry, she snapped, "Protection? Trust? Ha! You mean control and weakness is what you want of me. Well, you cannot manipulate me, Hawk. This wager will not be won so easily."

He froze. "The wager." His voice was flat and cold. "You think I am asking you to stay with me in order to manipulate the bet."

She swallowed back her emotions and nodded. "But I'm not your mistress to order about. You can't tell me where to live or what to do or who I can-"

Hawk cut her off with a shake of his head. "Perhaps sex is all you understand," he muttered beneath his breath before he closed the distance between them and backed her against the wall. He spun her so her breasts were flattened against the fancy wallpaper and his cock was pressed against her rear end. Already she could feel his swollen length nudging her gown and stroking the sensitive skin beneath.

"What are you doing?" she demanded, even though her true reaction was far from angry. His sudden forcefulness actually excited her. Her nipples tingled and she couldn't keep wet heat from shooting to her pussy.

He didn't answer as he shoved her skirt up and caressed her backside gently.

"Do you *ever* wear proper undergarments?" he breathed as he kissed the back of her neck.

She tried to remain cold, knowing this was his way of bending her to his will, but when she heard his trousers hit the floor in a heap and felt the hard thrust of skin on skin, a gush of wet warmth flowed to her loins.

"Hawk," she began on a short breath, intent on making some kind of protest, even a weak one.

He ignored her as he spread her wide and speared into her in one slow thrust. Bianca let out a moan despite herself as her body adjusted to take his thick length. He was heaven inside her, stretching her sensitive skin and filling her completely.

He braced his arms on each side of her head and pulled back inch by inch until he nearly left her body, then forward, just as slowly until his testicles tapped her backside. The pace was torture, awakening her with lazy ease, but never allowing her to find ultimate pleasure.

She pushed back against him in frustration, reaching for the release he wouldn't give her. But with a low laugh, he gripped her hips, imprisoning her with his superior strength to keep her from taking the lead.

"I will give you what you crave, if you give me what I crave," he murmured, licking a hot path from her ear to the junction of her shoulder and her neck.

"I'm trying, Hawk," she groaned as his thrust up into her again. Her body contracted, quivering on the very edge of a precipice. "You won't let me."

"Not that, Bianca. If you tell me you'll come to live here until our wager is over, I'll give you the pleasure you crave."

"Blackmail," she gasped as he rolled his hips in a slow circle.

"Incentive," he countered.

Bianca fought to keep a handle on her emotions and her mind. Her body screamed for her to tell him whatever he wanted to hear, but she couldn't surrender again. Not so soon after he'd bested her last night. And especially not when emotions had run so raw between them just moments before.

With a growl, she slid her hand off the wall and down the front of her body. With a few flicks of her fingers, she knew she would obtain what she craved. Only Hawk anticipated her. In a flash, he pinned her hands against the wall and withdrew to the head of his cock again. Only this time he held there, withholding his body, her pleasure, even her very sanity.

"Tell me you'll stay or I'll tie you to my bed and keep you on the brink of orgasm the whole night."

His voice was strained. Even without looking at him, she knew he was hurting himself as much as he was torturing her. But she also knew from experience that he would follow through on that threat. She wasn't sure she could take a night of pleasure so intense.

Her body tingled, throbbed and she bent her head in defeat. "Yes," she whispered. "I'll come and stay here with you. Now, please-!"

She didn't have to finish before Hawk slammed forward. She arched against him with a cry as they both slid down the wall. Now he knelt behind her body, thrusting with more purpose and intensity than before. She couldn't hold back the little cries as each thrust brought her closer and closer to powerful release.

Hawk grasped her hand, this time guiding her fingers down to her clit. Together they stroked the throbbing nub until finally, with a blast of hot wetness, she exploded. As if he'd been waiting for that moment, Hawk joined her in release, grasping her hips with all his might as they collapsed onto the rug before the fire.

Pinned beneath his heavy body, Bianca stared at the dancing flames as she listened to their breathing merge into one common rhythm. As amazing as that experience had been, she was furious with herself. Hawk had used her body against her yet again, forcing a promise from her that she hadn't wanted to give.

With a moan, she separated their bodies and rolled away. He flopped onto his back with a satisfied smile. Of course, he would be satisfied. He was winning their damned bet not two days after they'd begun!

She covered her eyes with her hands. She'd thought this would be easy, but Hawk simply wouldn't give in. She scowled up at the ceiling high above. The trick was to pull herself together, stop thinking with her clit and use Hawk's weaknesses against him just as handily as he used hers. He didn't have many, but it was obvious he wanted her.

She peeked between her fingers at him. Hawk had put his hands behind his head and crossed his bare ankles. He looked like he was napping. Napping!

But his cock was still awake. Even though he'd just spent, it was still at attention, ready for more.

Quietly, Bianca smoothed her skirts back over her naked lower body and crawled to Hawk's side. She grasped the base of his erection and wrapped her lips around him before he could protest.

"Bianca," he gasped.

She looked up. His eyes were wide open now, staring as she slowly worked her mouth up and down his steely shaft. With a smile, she made her job a show, darting out the tip of her pink tongue to stroke the underside, gliding her hand up and down in rhythm with her mouth. For once, she was in control. And Hawk was going to pay for forcing her hand not once, but twice.

She worked his cock with every bit of skill she had learned over the years, taking him to the edge of orgasm several times, but always backing away before he found his pleasure. A thin sheen of sweat glittered on his brow and his hips arched helplessly as she sucked and licked him to what she knew was the edge of madness.

But before she let him free, she popped his erection from her mouth and scrambled to her feet. Hawk's eyes went wide.

"What are you doing?" he gasped with a wild expression.

She strolled to the door, confident in the knowledge that with his pants feet away and his throbbing cock keeping him off guard, he wouldn't follow quickly enough to dole out punishment.

"I'm going home. If I'm coming back here to stay with you, I certainly need to prepare myself. Good evening."

She shut the door behind her with a sound click and enjoyed the echo of his howl of frustration as she headed for the exit and her waiting carriage.

Chapter Six

Hawk watched Bianca's wrinkled skirts disappear as she slammed the door behind her and flopped onto his back with a frustrated growl. However, he couldn't deny he was also impressed by her. For now, at least, this wager was a game and Bianca had just scored her first point.

His cock throbbed with unspent need and his blood rushed hot with desperation. Which was exactly what his adversary needed and desired.

He couldn't help his grin as he hooked his hand behind his head. Desperate or no, he had enjoyed every moment of their intense encounter.

Well, nearly every moment. He scowled as an image of Bianca's bruised face and arms twisted his gut. Firth would pay and pay dearly for daring to put his hands on her. No matter how much her rejection had crushed the man, it gave the bastard no right to brutalize her.

The fact that Firth had gone so far in such a public fashion was cause for even more alarm. If the man didn't care if Bianca's protective servants saw his attack, how much further would he have gone in private?

Hawk had little doubt Bianca was in more danger from her former lover than she cared to admit. Why she was so resistant to the protection he could provide, Hawk didn't know.

Except when it came to Bianca, resistance seemed to be a part of her very personality. Shutting his eyes, he pictured her. The image he conjured was clear and powerful. It also revealed something he had never marked before.

Bianca forever had distance in her stare. Even with a lover, even with Oscar…even with him. She invited and enticed with her body. She was wild and bold without fear of consequences, but behind the come-hither audacity, there was a glimmer of something else.

Pain.

There had been flashes of true emotions that sometimes bubbled to the surface when they were together, but he had never identified what those feelings were until that very moment.

His eyes flew open and Hawk surged to his feet. He shrugged into his discarded trousers and paced the room like a caged tiger. Why had he never recognized that pain before? God, he had practically been obsessed with the woman since the moment he met her. He had lost himself in the way she moved, the way her hair fell across her face, the way she smelled…

"Wait," he murmured as he stopped pacing at the window and stared outside with unseeing eyes. "That's it."

He had never taken note of Bianca's pain because she used her lush body like a shield. Her sensuality, her open, even blatant promises were simply weapons used to keep herself isolated. To control every situation and every man in the only way she knew how.

Sex.

Wager Of Sin

He winced as an overwhelming sadness crested in him. Bianca found pleasure, he had no doubt of that. But her pleasure was secondary to the protection and control she found in a man's bed.

Even his bed.

The thought that she kept him separate from her true self was hateful. Still, for the first few moments in the sitting room that night, her guard had been down. Her face had been drawn and emotional as she wrapped her arms around him and clung to him as if he was her lifeline. She had given him trust, if only briefly.

Hawk grabbed his shirt off the floor and shook it out absently. Bianca had given him an all-too-brief glimpse of herself.

He wanted more.

A shock went through his body at that admission. But it was true. He wanted more than her body for a month. He wanted more than to win the wager. He wanted to gain more of that precious trust Bianca withheld from everyone else in her life. He wanted to see her heart.

But it wouldn't be easy. She'd shown that already. He was torn by two objectives that seemed to oppose each other. To win the bet and keep Bianca in his life, he was forced to play her game of sexual warfare.

But to win her heart, he would have to show her there was more between them than simply the heat of sensual desire. That there was more to *her* than a protective shield of sex and sin.

He pulled his shirt over his shoulders with a new resolve. The only way to win Bianca was to know her past. To know her pains. Her secrets.

To know her in every way possible. Even if he had to fight her resistance every step of the way.

Even if he had to use her own weapons against her.

* * *

The door leading to Bianca's bedchamber opened as easily as every other entryway to the house had. No one had heard an intruder come in. No one had been on guard for an attack. And here in the shimmering moonlight, beneath her sheets, the outline of her body was as plain as if every candle in her room were lit.

Hawk shut the door quietly and leaned against it. His heart was racing and not only because the sight of Bianca made his blood hot. The ease of his forced entry only proved what he feared. Bianca was in too much danger from Everett Firth if she stayed in these walls.

His jaw set as rage pulsed through him. He could kill the bastard.

Slipping across the room in silence, he stopped at the foot of Bianca's bed. Her beauty hit him like a punch and set him off balance. But that beauty wasn't her only attribute. He wanted her for much more than the shell she showed the world.

Tonight he needed to gain back some of the ground she'd won from him with her skilled mouth. Gain back some ground and gently extract more of her trust… all while exacting a little sensual revenge in the process.

Hawk grabbed the edge of her coverlet and slowly pulled the blankets away from her body. When he saw she was nude, he had to bite his lip to keep from gasping out pleasure. Of course she would sleep naked. She hardly wore undergarments when she was awake.

He took a ginger perch on the edge of her bed. Bianca made a soft sigh in her throat and arched her back, but she didn't wake.

The fact that she was utterly helpless aroused Hawk. He liked that he could do anything he wished and make her wake in the thrashes of a powerful orgasm. The idea of that was far too intoxicating not to try.

He placed a gentle hand on each of her thighs and spread her legs. She moaned in her sleep, but still didn't wake. He thanked his luck that she was a deep sleeper. Her sex shone in the dim moonlight, wet though he'd barely touched her.

"What were you dreaming about?" he whispered as he slid down the bed between her legs.

Drawing a deep breath of her earthy, aroused fragrance, he spread the pouting outer lips of her pussy. Now her moans grew louder as she arched toward his seeking fingers. He bent his head and gave a languid lick from the bud of her clit all the way to the pinched hole on her bottom. Immediately she grew wetter and lolled her head to the side with a gasp.

Hawk's cock stretched as he went in for another stroke of his tongue. She tasted sweet and hot with unspent desire. Slowly, he glided one thick finger into her sheath, then another before he suckled her clit. He glided his fingers in and out of her clenching body as he darted his tongue over and over the tight core of her pleasure.

"Oh, Hawk," she moaned.

Startled, he lifted his head. Bianca's eyes were closed and her breathing remained heavy with sleep. She wasn't awake, she was simply dreaming. Dreaming the pleasure she so craved was being given by him.

His erection ached, but he didn't take her. He'd only do that when her eyes were open and she could watch him slide inside inch by inch. And the best way to make those beautiful blue eyes flutter to awareness was to make her come. He was sure the powerful pleasure of an orgasm would bring her to reality.

He strummed his tongue over her clit, pounding a hot tattoo of pressure and breath over her most sensitive spot. Finally, she arched up and let out a low, hungry cry. Her body spasmed around his hand and a gush of cream coated his fingers while she came.

As he had predicted, the moment her body twitched with release, her eyes flew open. As she cried out and gripped for her sheets, she glanced down at him in sleepy confusion.

"H-Hawk?" she stammered on a groan as her body wracked with tremors one last time. "I-I…"

He smiled as he rose from the bed. Leaning down, he pressed a hard, hot kiss on her lips and let her taste her own essence on his tongue.

"You're not dreaming," he murmured before he backed away to let her awaken fully and realize what had just happened. That he had pleasured her out of her slumber.

Bianca struggled to a sitting position to blink at him. "I-I don't understand." Her lips quirked up. "Not that I mind."

Her hand stirred as if to reach for him, but Hawk backed away. As much as he wished to take her, it had to wait. They were playing a dangerous game of control and surrender. One he had to win.

"You left me in a bit of a state earlier," he said and enjoyed the way she smiled triumphantly. "I thought I'd prove to you I can take you anywhere and anytime I like." He said the words evenly and slowly and watched her smile fade and high color enter her cheeks. "Even if you walk out of my sitting room and leave my erection ready to explode."

She swallowed. He watched her throat work and couldn't help but remember the feel of her lips on his member.

"Is that so?" It was obvious she meant for her tone to be challenging, but instead it came out as a squeak.

"I'm here, aren't I?" he asked as he walked to her fireplace. He tossed a few logs on the dying embers and the flames leapt up to brighten the room. "And I made you come without even waking you. I'd say it's so."

With a purse of her lips, she pulled the sheet up around her nude body. Hawk had to laugh at her grasp for control over the situation when he'd so readily proven he could and would take her despite her tactics to keep the upper hand.

"Actually, I was a little surprised not to find you sleeping in the master suite." He motioned his head toward the adjoining door to Oscar's old bedroom. He had searched there when he first arrived.

Bianca's eyes came up to look at the door, then she turned her head away with a small shrug. Hawk's hackles rose. They had never spoken of Oscar, partly because of his own guilt, but mostly because he hadn't wanted to hear about their happy marriage and passionate existence.

Now he had to hear the truth. As painful as that might be for him, it was the key to gaining her trust. To showing her she meant more to him than a warm body in his bed.

"Does it hurt you to talk about him?" he murmured as he let the fire's warmth ease into his suddenly cold skin.

"Hmm." She shrugged again. "I don't like that he died. It makes me sad to think his life was cut short by such a stupid accident."

Hawk flinched. If only she knew the truth…

"I wonder if you still love him." He said the words in an even tone, but inside a shot of pain rocked him. Why, he couldn't have said, or didn't want to. After all, Oscar had been her husband. Why wouldn't she miss him? Why wouldn't she mourn him?

"Love him?" Bianca pulled the sheet up ever further, protecting herself from him, as she always did. "I never loved Oscar and he certainly never loved me."

Hawk was glad he was leaning on her mantle. If he hadn't been, he might have fallen over in sudden surprise and delight at her answer.

"That sounds terrible, doesn't it?" Bianca shuffled on her bed with an uncomfortable glance in his direction. "Especially to you. You were so close to him."

Hawk shook his head. "No. Not terrible. Just surprising. You two always seemed so-so-" He stumbled for a word that wouldn't reveal how jealous he had always been.

"We *were* happy," she interrupted, freeing him from the chore of covering his real feelings. "Oscar was very open with me. On our honeymoon night, he told me a marriage with passion, but not love was the healthiest kind. He said no one got hurt in that equation. Two people could be friends and share pleasure in every way, but that they would avoid the petty jealousy and fighting that plagued so many marriages."

Hawk frowned. He could only imagine how Oscar's explanation must have hurt Bianca at the time, even if there was no pain now.

Her eyes took on a faraway distance. "Oscar awakened my body. He taught me about my sexuality and that pleasure wasn't the shame society said it was. And he pressed my boundaries and gave me absolute freedom to explore my deepest desires."

His eyes widened. He and Oscar had talked about their sexual conquests, but Bianca had remained off limits. Now his cock stirred as he pictured her sexual awakening. And wished he had been the one to give it to her.

"How?" he asked in a hoarse whisper as he moved from the mantle to the foot of the bed and sat down.

Bianca arched an eyebrow, but her eyes sparkled. He could see remembering the decadence of her past also awakened fresh desire in her. She let the sheet slip down suggestively and looked him straight in the eyes.

"Oscar taught me how to touch myself," she said quietly. "He brought a mirror to the bed and let me examine myself while he touched me so I would know which spots brought me the most pleasure."

Hawk shifted, but it didn't relieve the desire caused by her words and the powerful images that accompanied them.

"He would spend hours making love to me in the beginning." She rubbed her neck seductively. "And he'd concentrate on one spot for so long. The shell of my ear. The slope of my neck. My nipples. My thighs. Sometimes I'd be trembling for him by the time he finally entered me. But it was all part of his education. That pleasure was sometimes about waiting. Giving. And sometimes it was about taking and immediacy."

She looked at Hawk for a long moment before she dropped the sheet around her waist. Her rosy nipples were puckered and hard.

"And then he introduced me to pleasures so dark and scandalous no one ever talks about them. He brought other women to our bed, other men. He would watch as another woman bathed me, touched me. Then he would take us in turn.

"I loved every moment of the passion we shared." She gave him a shaky smile. "But I didn't love him."

Hawk shivered. He had never been so hard in all his life as he was now. His cock throbbed, aching to delve into her perfumed heat and rut until she forgot all the nights that she'd spent with other men. Because as much as the images aroused him, the idea of her sharing her body with someone else awakened a jealousy in him he'd never experienced.

He wanted her to pleasure him alone. To be pleasured by him alone. Unlike Oscar, he wasn't willing to share. But he did want to introduce her to new ecstasies. Including ones that had nothing to do with sex.

"The only thing Oscar didn't do was dominate me," she said with a pointed glare for Hawk. "He was far kinder than you in that regard."

Hawk rose from the bed and tossed his jacket aside. Bianca straightened as she watched him strip the remainder of his clothing off piece by piece.

He crawled up beside her on the bed and grabbed her waist to slip her beneath his hard, ready body. She let out a little gasp, but didn't fight.

"You like it when I dominate you," he said softly before he nipped her lips.

"No." She shook her head, but even as her eyes fluttered shut with pleasure. "I like being in control."

"Then why do you strain against me when I hold you down?" Hawk asked, proving his point by pinning her hands over her head. Immediately her pelvis tilted against his and she blushed.

He dragged the back of his hand down over her collarbone, between the swell of her breasts, then back and forth over the globes until her nipples swelled and darkened with desire.

"Why do you beg me so sweetly when I won't let you control everything?" he asked before he let his hand slip between her legs. As he had suspected, she was still wet from his mouth and the fresh flow of need as she'd told him about her decadent sex life with Oscar.

"I can make you come like this." He flicked his wrist, touching her clit in just the right way that her eyes rolled back in her head as she achieved a tiny release.

"Or like this." This time he rubbed the head of his cock over her clit. Back and forth, up and down, pressing down with enough pressure that her orgasm increased and she couldn't hold back a plaintive moan.

"And that." He continued to toy with her, never penetrating, but finding new ways to make her come. Each time the orgasm was harder, more intense, until she was panting and writhing.

"Please, Hawk." Her voice was small as she strained up against him. "Please. Put your cock in me. I need it."

He let his hand glide back up to cup her chin and held her stare evenly. "You need *me*."

Blue eyes flashed with defiance, but her desperation proved more powerful. "Tonight, I need you."

He smiled. Despite the fact that he was trying to win her surrender, Hawk loved her rebellious streak. It made her interesting. It made her Bianca. And once he had won her, he would encourage her at every turn.

But tonight he needed to take her.

He spread her legs wide, draping one over each of his shoulders. In the vulnerable position, she couldn't control the pace of their lovemaking. With a sigh, he plunged into her softness. He reveled in the pulse of her inner walls, the way her body stretched to allow him to fill her to capacity.

When he drew back, she clung to him with humid heat, stroking his cock with her pussy until he thought he'd go mad with waiting. But it was only when her back arched and her cries filled the room that he let go of control and filled her with his seed. A final claim that she was his.

And if he had his way, she always would be.

Chapter Seven

Bianca rung her hands. Despite the warm summer air that blew in through the open window in her father's parlor, her fingers were ice cold with anxiety.

When he'd sent word he wanted to see her, Bianca thought of refusing him, but she couldn't. He was her father. Despite his misguided fears and her own anger, she knew he loved her and she refused to create a permanent estrangement between them by avoiding him. Even though she feared she might be walking into a trap every time she saw him.

She sent a side glance toward the door, afraid he would walk in with a barrister who would declare her unfit and immediately drag her kicking and screaming to her old bedroom... her prison.

Unable to control her worry any longer, Bianca jumped to her feet and paced to the window. It overlooked her father's beautiful gardens. They had always brought her peace, but not today. Today she wondered how soon this house would become her jail cell.

"Are the rumors true?"

She spun around as her father stormed into the room and slammed the door behind him, right in the face of their old butler. He didn't seem to care that every servant in the house was to be privy to their disagreement. Something that proved things had deteriorated a great deal since their last discussion when he had worked to keep their arguments private.

She forced a smile. "Good morning, Papa, you're looking well."

"Are you living at Lucius Hawkins' town home?" he asked in a harsh, loud tone that seemed to crackle in the air as if a whip was being snapped.

Bianca dipped her head. Their new living arrangements had been the talk of London for the last week. For the most part, she didn't care about the gossip and censure, but seeing the disapproval in her father's face both angered and pained her.

She jutted her chin up with defiance. "Yes. I have my reasons, Father."

"Your reasons?" he repeated before he slammed a fist against her mother's antique sideboard. Glass tinkled as it shivered and shook. Bianca had never seen him so angry before. "Don't talk to me about your reasons! You don't know the meaning of the word 'reason'."

She shook her head. "Father, it's my life. I understand you don't approve of any of this and it hurts me greatly to know what a disappointment I am to you and my brothers. Despite what you may think, I do care for you all very deeply and my last wish would be to bring you pain."

His eyes softened. "Then please, Bianca, please. Come home. It is probably too late to salvage what's left of your reputation here in London, but I could send you to the country. At least you would have your family."

She laughed. Didn't he understand that by forcing this issue, he was going to make her lose everything? *Including* her family.

"Papa, I can't change who I am. I won't." She drew a harsh breath. "And you are the last one who should ask me to. After all, you helped make me this way."

A heavy, permeating silence filled the room as her father's face darkened to a deep red. He opened his mouth and shut it wordlessly a few times until she actually took a step toward him in worry.

Before she reached him, he set his jaw. The implacable glint in his eye stopped her.

"How dare you imply I have been a party to your shameful decline and decadent lifestyle?"

She shook her head. For years she had hidden her anger, but now that she was being threatened it bubbled to the surface.

"No, father, you have been as much a party to the life I lead as I have been."

"How?" he barked.

"You insisted I enter into a marriage with Oscar. *You* handed me over to a man with such appetites."

"I knew nothing of..." Her father blushed and stammered. "His-his appetites or I surely would not have given my innocent daughter over to him."

She sighed as her anger fizzled. "But you did turn me over to him. And you cannot blame me for finding a way to survive in my marriage. For finding a way to live, not in horror, but in acceptance. Even pleasure after a time."

"Oscar is dead now."

She laughed. "Yes, but I am changed irrevocably. My marriage altered me, I couldn't return to being that 'innocent' girl even if I wished to."

"You could try!" he cried.

"No." She shook her head with a long sigh. "I won't go back to having no choices about my own fate."

Her father's eyes filled with exhaustion and suddenly he looked far older than his years.

"Don't force my hand, child." His voice was barely above a whisper.

With tears pricking her eyes, she crossed to his side and took his rough hand in hers. Suddenly she realized just how much she would lose if she were forced to flee to the Continent. Her family, her home, her friends… and Hawk.

"Don't force mine."

He reached up to cup her cheek and for a moment she saw the look of pure love she'd always seen as a child. "I could call the bastard out," he said without any heat in his voice.

She pursed her lips as she moved away. "Oh, Papa. You would kill another man? You would have me declared unfit and lock me away from the life I've chosen to lead? You would do these things and call it protection and love?"

He nodded emphatically. "Yes! You're throwing away your life and what's left of your good name. If you come back here, you could go into seclusion for a few years. Afterward, I would find you a new husband. Someone calm. Suitable."

She threw up her hands in utter frustration. "So you would decide my future for me… again? And what if this man you chose was just like Oscar? Or even worse? He could abuse me. He could be cruel where Oscar was simply selfish."

Blue fire flashed in the eyes that looked so much like her own. "But you could rejoin society!"

"I don't give two figs about society. They talk up their sleeves about me and my life, but they continue to invite me to their parties. They say it's out of respect to you and my late husband, but in reality it's because I fascinate them. Even if they refused me, it wouldn't matter."

She picked up her gloves from the table where she'd set them and began to pull them back on finger by finger. "What I have learned in the years since my marriage is that I only have one life. I want to live it, not watch it from my perfect little perch in a sitting room. Not let you or anyone else dictate who I keep company with and what I do."

"Damn it, girl! I can't let this go on much longer." He followed her to the door with a sigh of frustration.

She dipped her head. With everything in her heart and soul, she knew he was motivated by the best of intentions. Yet those intentions would destroy her.

"Goodbye."

Without looking at him, she walked to the foyer door and outside into the sunshine. She barely felt her footman help her inside and the carriage start to rumble. She cast one last glance out the window at her father. He stood on his front veranda, his eyes sad as she pulled away from him.

The tears she forced herself to hide began to fall, trickling down her cheeks and into the handkerchief she had retrieved from her reticule.

There were only two men in her life she couldn't bend to her will. One who wanted to destroy her world, and the one who could save her.

Wiping her eyes, Bianca tapped on the wall that separated her from her driver. He came to a stop as a footman appeared in the window.

"Yes, my lady?"

"Take me to Madame Deville's," she ordered as she settled back against the cushioned seat.

It was time to settle this matter with Hawk for once and for all.

* * *

It had been a long time since Bianca had been in Madame Clarissa Deville's Den of Sensuality, but in the years since Oscar's death, the place hadn't changed. The décor was still done in red satin and velvet, from the rich wall hangings to the opulent furnishings. Everything was meant to be soft and rich and seductive.

Clarissa's 'girls' had different faces now, but it seemed they were the same women dressed in negligees and elaborate costumes to fit any gentleman's fantasy. None of them had the haggard, empty look some women of their profession exhibited. Bianca supposed it was because Madame took good care of her charges.

Bianca stood in the front parlor waiting for Clarissa and watching a couple in the corner. The gentleman wasn't particularly handsome, but the swell of his erection that ballooned his trousers was enormous as the beautiful woman on his lap gyrated over him in tiny little circles. Her bosom was almost overflowing from the thin expanse of black lace covering it.

It was apparent that within moments the two would retire to one of Madame's bedrooms to finish their transaction, but Bianca was enjoying the show until that moment came.

The first time Oscar brought her here it had been different. After months of marriage, she had already moved passed the initial shock Oscar's sexual appetites and demands had caused. She'd come to accept her own sensuality and even enjoy the intense encounters she shared with her husband.

But here, within these walls, he had pushed her boundaries mercilessly. She had watched the whores with their men and horror had again coursed through her. But Oscar hadn't allowed her to leave. As she had so many times, she separated her mind from the events around her.

But Oscar had insisted they bring Clarissa into their bed that night. She had wept. But over many nights she had come to accept the new arrangements. Even though it hurt her to do so. Even though it had broken her heart that she wasn't enough for the man she called husband.

Even now she shivered with the memory and the harsh feelings it brought up. The emotions she worked so hard to tamp down and erase. The ones that made her weak.

"Madame Clarissa will see you now," the butler said.

Bianca shook away her troubling thoughts as she followed the man up the stairs. On the way, she passed another gentleman coming down. He was patting his red brow with a handkerchief and looked well satisfied. Obviously Clarissa still knew how to please her clientele.

The butler opened the door to Clarissa's chamber and motioned Bianca in.

"There you are, my dear," Clarissa said as she came out from behind a changing screen, tying her robe around her waist. "I was so surprised and delighted to hear you were visiting me."

Bianca kissed her on each cheek with a smile. "It's been a long time."

"Before Oscar's death." Clarissa's face fell.

Bianca sighed with a nod. It was no secret the other woman had cared deeply for Oscar. Sometimes Bianca wondered if she'd been a little in love with him.

"I wish you had come to his funeral," Bianca said as Clarissa sat down at a mirrored table and began to wash her smeared make-up off. "He would have liked you to be there."

Clarissa smiled sadly. "Come, my dear. You and I know a gentleman may play in my world, but I must never invade his. My coming would have caused a terrible scene." She paused. "I did go visit his grave later. I hope you don't mind."

Bianca reached out to touch Clarissa's shoulder and their eyes met in the mirror. "Of course not. I'm glad you did."

Clarissa tossed her a warm smile, then went back to her work. "Now why did you come? I can see by your eyes that this isn't simply a call to reminisce with an old friend." Bianca laughed as she sank down into one of Clarissa's deep, cushy chairs. "I admit, I've come to ask for your advice."

Clarissa spun to face Bianca. Her eyes were wide and her mouth dipped open. "*You*, ask my advice? Well, this is interesting. Not only were you one of the most sensual women who ever came into my establishment, but I've heard a great deal about your escapades since you came out of mourning."

She shrugged. "Normally I haven't required any expert advice. But I've become involved with a man who is difficult to tame. I've been struggling to bend him to my will."

"Ha!" Her friend shook her head. "I doubt that. No man wouldn't bend to your will. I think you could have made even Oscar come to heel if you'd put much effort into the exercise."

Bianca folded her arms. "This is no ordinary man. It's Lucius Hawkins."

Clarissa's eyes widened to an almost painful looking degree and for a long time she was silent. Then she let out her breath in a long whistle. "By God, you do pick well. First Oscar and then his best friend. Hawk is one of the most talented bed partners…"

She forced a smile, but an increasingly strong flash of jealousy surprised Bianca. She'd actually shared her husband with this woman and though she had felt pain, it had never been the pangs of jealousy, but inadequacy. Eventually, she actually enjoyed watching Oscar take Clarissa.

But knowing the courtesan had taken Hawk to her bed made Bianca want to slap her. It was such a powerful reaction it surprised her.

"Yes, he's quite talented," she managed through clenched teeth. "But how do I tame him? I need him to be desperate. He must beg for me, be addicted to me."

"Hawk? Good luck."

Bianca pursed her lips. Her ire about this situation was steadily increasing. She couldn't explain her powerful reaction to Clarissa's intimate knowledge. She had purged jealousy and possessiveness from her nature. Why she felt them when it came to Hawk was beyond her.

"Well, your faith in me is heartwarming," she snapped. "The questions is, can you help me if you're such an expert in men and Hawk in particular?"

Clarissa got to her feet and arched an eyebrow at Bianca's tone. She examined her face with a little smile that made Bianca's heart race. Then she shrugged.

"The only way to make a man that powerful become desperate is to take away his control. His control is tied to his physical strength and ability to dominate you. Steal that strength and he'll be at your mercy."

Bianca's heart raced as she thought of how often Hawk had dominated her. Time and time again, he had taken her carefully cultivated power, then used it to draw secrets from her. To stoke emotions she was better off never feeling again.

She had to regain that advantage. Not just for the bet, but for her own sanity.

"How?" she murmured.

Clarissa crossed her room to a bureau by her door. She opened the bottom drawer and pulled out four long, velvet ropes. Dangling them out toward Bianca, she asked, "Did you and Oscar ever play at bondage games?"

She stared at the ropes as she shook her head. "No. He told me about them, of course, but he liked to have my hands free."

Clarissa smiled knowingly. "Then this will be a new adventure for you. I suggest you tie him down as soon as you get a chance. Use your most trusted servants to help you if you must. Once he is secured, you'll be free to torture him all you like. I venture he'll be desperate and begging if you toy with him long enough. After all, he *is* a man."

Bianca laughed as she took the ropes. The velvet caressed her fingers and sent a jolt of hot awareness through her.

"You are a genius, my friend. No wonder you're so popular," she said with a laugh. For the first time since Hawk dominated her so completely, she was beginning to feel optimistic about her chances in the wager.

"I'm certainly glad I can help." Clarissa smiled. "Now, go. You'll have preparations to make if you plan to use those tonight."

Bianca nodded, gave her friend a quick kiss on the cheek and hurried to the door. Only Clarissa's voice stopped her.

"Bianca?"

She turned back. "Yes?"

"If you ever want to share again, let me know."

Bianca paled at the thought of sharing Hawk with the beautiful concubine. It actually hurt her.

Clarissa smiled at her silent horror. "You know, my dear, those ropes won't keep him from your heart."

Bianca faltered at her friend's clear vision. "My heart? Don't be silly. I wouldn't waste my time on love."

She hurried from the room before Clarissa could dissect any more of her soul. It was only in the carriage that she realized Clarissa had never said anything about love.

Chapter Eight

"This evening your supper will be served in your bedchamber, sir."

Hawk stared with a blank expression at the footman he didn't recognize, while another equally strange servant took his coat. "The bedroom? I'm sorry, who are you?"

"Lady Bianca gave your servants the night off," the young man explained with a bow before he motioned Hawk toward the stairs. "And asked us, her own servants, to prepare a special supper and serve you. In your room, sir."

Hawk's cock stirred. He liked the sound of this. Bianca had certainly been busy since they reluctantly parted ways that morning so she could tend to some family business.

It pleased him that she had arranged an unexpected evening for him. Yet he wondered if there was something more sinister behind it. Since her arrival in his home, she had continued to struggle against his will, even though she always ended up yielding to him so sweetly in the end.

Perhaps there was no ulterior motive. He could only hope she was simply beginning to lower the high walls she erected around herself. That her acquiescence was moving beyond her body to something deeper.

One of Bianca's footmen opened the door to his chamber. Hawk stopped in the doorway with a gasp of surprise. Hundreds of candles flickered from all corners of the room and a blazing fire warmed him even from the doorway. A small table had been put in the center of the floor and was ready with covered dishes and even more candles.

"My God," he murmured as he entered the room. "Bianca?"

She stepped from the only darkened corner of the room silently and gave him a charming, but nervous smile. Her hair, as black as her silky, sheer wrapper, was piled on her head in a casual, sensual pile. Hawk longed to slide the robe from her shoulders and just suck on her long, gorgeous neck for a few hours.

Instead, he motioned around the room and asked, "Is this for me?"

She laughed. "Of course! Please, sit down."

He took the chair she motioned to and she sat beside him. "I wanted to do something special tonight. I hope you don't mind that I excused your servants."

He shook his head as one of her men revealed hot bowls of soup from beneath metal covers. "Of course not. I like that you've made these elaborate plans for me. Though I do wonder at your motives." He tossed her a wink and she returned a saucy one of her own.

"My motives are clear enough, aren't they?" she asked with innocence he knew not to trust.

"Never," he laughed. "I never know what you're thinking, but I wouldn't have it any other way."

Reaching out, he caught her hand with his own and held it up to his lips. He darted his tongue out to caress the sensitive webbing between her fingers and was rewarded by her gasp and the very obvious hardening of her nipples beneath the thin, gauzy wrap.

"I-I suppose I'm glad to keep you off balance if that's what you like," she said with a coy smile. But beneath the expression, he saw how much he affected her. For a woman with such vast experience with lovers, her reactions remained disingenuous and spontaneous. Hawk loved that dichotomy. It was a fleeting glimpse of her true self.

As the footmen presented the next course of their meal, he watched Bianca. Tonight she was different. Her beauty in her simple hairstyle and scandalously sheer wrap was amazing. But beyond that, he was being treated to a taste of her gentility. She was the perfect hostess as she served him wine and quietly directed her footmen about courses and other matters. It gave Hawk a glimpse of the lady she still was beneath her untamed and wanton exterior.

The lady she surrendered in trade for a life of shocking sensuality. But her gentility came so easily it was clear she once planned for a more traditional life. Her open, sexually charged existence with Oscar had probably shocked the proper girl she'd once been. Slowly, she had surrendered her own dreams. Her own plans.

And found whatever power she could in her body.

But watching her, he found he liked the lady as much as he liked the wild woman who swept into his life like a storm at sea.

"You went out today?" he asked, allowing himself to pretend, just for a moment, that they were a normal couple sharing their supper.

Her fork faltered on its way to her plate, but she recovered quickly. "Yes. My father demanded my presence."

Hawk frowned at the sudden nervous tension in her expression. Though he knew very few details, it was clear the relationship between Bianca and her father was terribly strained. Even more obvious was how much that strain hurt her.

He touched her hand lightly. "It's difficult, I know."

She smiled and it softened the lines of her face. "Yes. You do know. You and your father were at odds before his death, weren't you? And you avoid your brother at all costs. Oscar once told me you refuse to go to parties if you discover Landon will be there."

Hawk nodded though the mention of his older brother sent a shot of angry pain through him. Since their father's death three years ago, Landon had taken over both his father's title and his contempt of Hawk. The two rarely spoke except when forced into the same room by their mother, who loved them and wanted to see them reconcile. Hawk didn't have the heart to tell her that it wasn't going to happen. He couldn't cope with his brother's overbearing opinions and orders.

Landon didn't seem to understand Hawk had made himself into an independent man. He no longer bowed to the Hawkins purse strings. His brother's highhanded disapproval often spurned Hawk to seek out activities that shocked his brother's high and mighty sensibilities.

Still, he sometimes longed for the days of their youth, when the brothers had been friends.

"I would hate to see you go through such an estrangement," Hawk said with a sigh. "Especially since your father and brothers obviously love you a great deal."

"They told you that while making threats on your life at Lady Langley's party, no doubt," she said in a dry tone.

Hawk laughed. "You know them well."

Her smile fell inexplicably. "Yes, too well. They are misguided in their belief that I need their protection. And my family will do anything to keep me under their wing." She seemed to go to a faraway place for a long moment. "Anything."

Hawk wrinkled his brow. He hated to see that quiver in her lower lip and the distance in her eyes. More than anything, he wanted to take both away.

"After you saw your family, did you do anything else?" he asked in an attempt to change the obviously painful subject.

Bianca's eyes came back in sharp focus on his face. "No," she snapped a little louder than he'd expected.

Hawk arched an eyebrow. "Visiting old lovers, were we?" he teased, though the thought of such a thing stung him.

Her smile was brittle. "You know me better than that, Hawk. I am a faithful mistress... unless my lover wishes me to make love with another."

His eyes fluttered shut at that thought. How could Oscar have watched his wife in bed with another man and find that arousing? Observing Bianca as she found pleasure was one of the greatest aphrodisiacs in the world. Hawk was growing more addicted to it every day, every hour. But he didn't know that he could bring himself to share her with anyone else.

"I don't wish that of you," he murmured as he looked at her through heavy lids.

"Good," she whispered.

The quiver in her tone drew Hawk's attention. Her demeanor when she told her story about her sexual adventures with Oscar and other lovers had implied she didn't mind. But her expression now belied that assertion.

Bianca wanted faithfulness.

And that gave him enormous hope.

With her slight nod, the footmen cleared away the rest of their plates. She leaned back in her chair. "Did you get enough?"

Hawk stirred as he looked at her from head to toe. In the firelight he saw the faint outline of her nipples through her dressing gown and the darker shadow of the soft hair between her legs. His body lurched with excitement he could no longer control.

"To eat?" He leaned forward to set a hand on the gentle slope of her knee.

She swallowed hard at the passing graze of his touch. "Yes."

"Of food, yes." He gave her a suggestive smile she very clearly understood, by the way her body stirred in response.

"And to drink?"

He tilted his head. Why the inquisition?

"Yes," he said slowly.

"Very good." She motioned over her shoulder to the three footmen who still stood in wait at the door. "Tom, Richard, Andrew, will you please finish here?"

Hawk opened his mouth, but before he could utter a word, the three men crossed the room like lightening and grabbed him. They wrenched his arms back as Hawk barked out a curse and struggled against the unexpected and unprovoked attack.

"What the hell is this?" he howled as they hauled him off the chair. His foot caught the edge of the table and it flipped, sending dishes and wine clattering across the floor. Bianca barely leapt out of the way as she hurried to her feet.

The men yanked him toward the bed. Hawk fought as hard as he could, but he was no match for the three of them together.

"Bianca!" he barked, but her face remained immoveable except for a tiny, knowing smile. She folded her arms and suddenly everything became shockingly, painfully clear.

"Strip him, if you would," she ordered calmly, as if she'd asked the men to bring them another bottle of wine.

Hawk bellowed in rage, but in a matter of moments, he'd been stripped to his bare ass and thrown onto the bed. He kicked and attempted to throw a few punches, but none of them even approached an effective defense as the footmen easily dodged his wild blows.

"The ties." Bianca almost sounded bored as she said the last two words.

Hawk's eyes widened as they flew to the bedposts. He hadn't noticed when he came in, but there were four velvet ropes, one on each post. With a few turns and twists, the men bound his wrists and ankles, then stood up and backed away, leaving him spread helplessly across his bed.

Bianca nodded with grim determination. "He's secure?"

"Yes, my lady," one of her goons said with a grin in Hawk's direction. "He ain't goin' no where until you let him."

"Thank you, gentlemen. You may collect this mess and go. And tell the others I won't require their service any more tonight. As soon as you've finished here, you may return home."

"Thank you, my lady."

Bianca stood at the foot of the bed watching Hawk as the servants collected the plates and empty bottles scattered on the floor.

Hawk resisted the urge to fight. He refused to show strangers that he was incensed by his helplessness. Even if he could loosen his ties, with them still in the room he would be quickly corralled and back in the same position. It was best to wait and let Bianca be the recipient of his frustration and the punishment he would dole out as soon as he was free.

Finally, the door closed and they were alone. Bianca's little smile stole Hawk's composure and he growled in frustration.

"What is this?" he bellowed.

She stepped closer, her eyes moving over him. Her expression was greedy, like a child suddenly let loose in a sweet shop without supervision. His anger bled away, replaced by a titillation that swelled his cock against his will.

Bianca glanced down at his lengthening member with a wider smile. "I think that's obvious, my dear," she murmured. Her tone was low and husky. It struck a chord in Hawk's body that made him stiffen even further.

She placed one finger on the coverlet beside him and ran a fingernail parallel to his leg. Hawk squirmed as he leaned toward her. His body ached for her touch.

"What the hell are you doing?" he repeated, but the heat in his voice was no longer the fire of anger.

"I am finally having my way," she whispered. "You wouldn't give it to me, so I've been forced to take it."

He watched in fascination as she slowly untied the knot on her wrap. She opened it bit by bit until it slipped off her shoulders to fall in a pool at her feet. Hawk gasped. He had seen her naked many times since their wager began. Each time her body still aroused him and her beauty still moved him.

By this point in most of his conquests he was tired of the women in his bed. Not Bianca. If anything, he felt like he was only at the cusp of discovering her secrets. And he wanted more.

"Bianca," he whispered.

She reached out and pressed two fingers against his lips as she crawled up on the bed to straddle his chest. The moist heat of her pussy gave his stomach a humid kiss and he hissed out pleasure as her thighs tightened around his sides.

"Shhh," she murmured as she carefully removed the pins from her hair. It fell around them like a black cloud, teasing his sensitive skin and filling his senses with exotic scent. "I wouldn't want to gag you, as well. No more arguments. I'm in control tonight."

Hawk growled as she slowly slid down his body, but it turned to a harsh moan when she let her nether lips pass over his swollen erection. The wet heat of her grasped him temporarily, then left him cold and throbbing as she glided between his legs.

Bianca looked up at him, meeting his eyes with a stare of blue heat. She dipped her head and licked the sensitive skin of his inner thigh. Hawk bit his lip to keep from crying out. Bianca wasn't going to have all the control.

"Mmm," she murmured. "You are delicious and I didn't have any dessert." She arched an eyebrow at his pained expression. "Do you know what I'm going to do?"

His lips thinned as she started massaging his hips gently.

"Ask me," she ordered.

"What are you going to do?" he ground out through clenched teeth.

"First I'm going to suck your cock until you can't control yourself and you come. Then I'm going to make you hard again and ride you." Her breath came short and her eyes never left his. "And you won't be able to do anything about it because tonight you are mine to do with as I please. And before the night is over... *you* will be the one begging."

He shut his eyes as her hot breath came down on his cock, followed by her wet lips. Grasping the base, she let her tongue glide over the head, swirling the sensitive peak with long licks. Hawk couldn't stop from groaning with pleasure. She smiled against his cock and went back to work in earnest.

He shivered when she took him deeply into her throat, then worked him back to the head over and over. Her rhythm was slow and steady, meant to take him to the edge, but keep him from going over until she was ready for his seed.

When she gently nipped his cock, Hawk jumped and strained against the velvet binds. To his surprise, one of them loosened just a fraction.

All the binds had been tied tightly except one. With a few subtle tugs, he could easily be free.

Bianca rolled her tongue around and around the shaft of his swollen penis. Hawk bit back a cry. Her mouth felt so good on him. If he stayed bound, he could surrender. The rewards of her skillful tongue and lips would be many. He had no doubt she would follow through on her promise to drain him, then bring him to a ready state again.

With difficulty, he opened his eyes and looked down at Bianca. Her eyes were closed and her hips thrust in time with her mouth as she pinioned her head up and down in slow rhythm on his cock. Her nipples were dark and hard. She was as excited by pleasuring him as he was.

It was a tempting prospect. Yet in the end, his surrender could mean his downfall. Both in their wager and beyond. The last thing he wanted to do was prove to her that all her power came through sex.

If only he could be strong a little longer, the rewards would be much higher. As his mistress, he would enjoy not only the pleasures of her body, but spend more time in her arms and in her life.

Ultimately, the moment's pure pleasure could wait until he had won her.

He tugged on the loose rope surreptitiously, straining as she worked him ever closer to completion with her sure, wet licks. Hawk's vision began to blur as his seed moved within him, straining to burst into her hot mouth.

With a cry, he yanked the bind free.

Bianca's head came up with a gasp. She let out a little scream as he used his free hand to wrench away the three other binds. She scrambled off the bed and nearly fell on her shapely rear end. But Hawk was already off the bed, right at her heels and ready to dole out the punishment that most definitely fit her crime.

Vengeance would be sweet, indeed.

* * *

The blood drained from Bianca's face so rapidly, she feared she might lose consciousness. Hawk had already proven he would pleasure her whether she was awake or not and she needed all her faculties to deal with the vengeful passion that turned his eyes from gray to black.

"Hawk… Hawk…" she managed to push through trembling lips as she backed toward the door with hands raised to ward him off.

He kept coming, step by step, with a possessive, dark smile on his face and his erection jutting toward her. It gleamed in the firelight with the moisture from her mouth.

"Begging, are we, Bianca?" he asked with a husky laugh. "I'm afraid there will be no mercy for you now."

She shook her head as she contemplated racing out of the room. But she wouldn't get far stark naked and she had a sneaking suspicion Hawk could and would easily outrun her. With no servants left in the house to interfere on her behalf, she had no chance.

So she was trapped in a prison of her own design and her heart raced as she contemplated what kind of sensual torture would be her punishment.

"Hawk!" she squealed as he finally lunged for her. His arms wrapped like vices around her waist, biding her arms helplessly to her sides. Her naked breasts rasped against his crisp chest hair and his cock bumped between her thighs as he spun on his heel. He carried her as if she was nothing more than a rag doll to the bed and tossed her unceremoniously onto the coverlet. She tried to flip over from her stomach to her back, but he threw his weight onto her and held her down as he stretched one of her arms out toward the bedpost.

He caught the bind and slipped her hand through it as he leaned down and pressed his lips against her exposed neck. "Velvet," he murmured as he stroked his tongue against the sensitive skin behind her ear. "Very nice."

"Hawk," she croaked out and was furious that his name was a moan from her lips. She had him where she wanted him, but in just a moment he not only burst free from her trap, but regained the power he always wielded over her. And now she was in the position she was always in with Hawk.

Submissive.

He tied her hands and feet, but it was obvious he was being careful not to hurt her. Somehow the care he took in making sure she couldn't escape, but wouldn't be injured, made her blood rush harder and hotter.

Tied face down on her bed, he could do anything to her. For the first time, she truly had no recourse.

And the thought was utterly thrilling though it went against every rule she made for herself over the past few years.

"You have been a very naughty girl," he said as he rose up on his knees. He cupped her rear end with large, hot hands. His fingers stroked over her sensitive flesh, dipping down between the globes to play over her pussy and ass.

He slipped a finger across her slit and she jolted with uncontrolled desire.

"Please, Hawk," she began, knowing if she begged she would be given release. "Let me come."

To her surprise, he shook his head with a laugh. "Oh, no. It won't be that easy tonight. You've earned far more punishment than a little teasing. By the time I'm finished, your body is going to be weeping with desire. And when I finally do take you, you'll explode like you never have before."

Already a sob escaped her lips at the heat of his promise and the empty clenching of her wanton body. She balled her useless hands into fists and waited for him to touch her again.

It wasn't long before he did. His hands came down on her thighs, parting them wider. His thumbs brushed her sex purposefully and she let out a long sigh. He bent his head and speared his tongue into her pussy without warning. Bianca bucked up with a wail as he mercilessly licked her. Heat spread from his tortuous tongue through her blood stream until she was a melted puddle of heat and desire.

Still, he went on and on, lapping at her from anus to clit and ignoring her gasps and pleas for release.

His tongue strokes became shorter and more focused on the sensitive hole of her bottom. Bianca gasped as Hawk glided his tongue over and over the opening. She never realized her rear end was so sensitive, or that touching and licking it could feel so decadent. Her clit throbbed with each wet stroke and she arched up reflexively.

"Did Oscar ever do this?" Hawk asked between tongue strokes.

"No," she gasped. "No one has ever done that."

"Good." Then he paused and placed a finger against the little hole. Lubricated by his mouth, the digit slid inside easily.

Stars exploded before Bianca's eyes at this foreign invasion. It was like losing her virginity all over again, but instead of the sharp and fleeting pain that had accompanied her wedding night, this was only bliss. Hawk slowly inched his finger in and out, stretching her and readying her for something else.

His cock. He hadn't said it, but his long, hard erection would feel even better than his thick finger.

"This will feel strange," he said in a tense voice as he positioned himself behind her and pressed the round head of his penis against her. "But I promise I won't hurt you."

"Please," she whimpered. "I want to feel it. To feel you."

She pushed back against him and his cock slid inside a few inches. Hawk gripped her hips and moaned long and low.

"Wait," he whispered. "Slowly or I'll hurt you."

Bianca moaned. "It's too slow. I need all of you."

Hawk reached around her body and cupped her breasts as he inched his cock inside her rear end with slow, short thrusts. Each forward motion spread her even further, and made her tender nerves fire with pleasure so intense and focused it was almost pain. She bucked in time, forcing him inside, farther and farther until he was imbedded to the very hilt.

Her pussy clenched at nothing, shivering on the cusp of an orgasm even though he hadn't touched her clit or filled her sheath. Just the fullness of him in this new and dark place made her quiver with pleasure she'd never felt before.

"Am I hurting you?" he asked against her back.

"No. I just want more."

With a growl, he pulled back and began to thrust, slow and even inside her. She mewled with pleasure, arching as far as her bound hands would let her and curling her toes.

"You're so tight, so hot," he gasped as his hands massaged her breasts with almost wild intensity.

"Don't punish me anymore," Bianca cried as her body reached the breaking point of pleasure. "Let me come."

Hawk stopped moving and she wailed in frustration as the pleasure that had been peaking in her diminished to a low, insistent throb. He reached up and unbound each of her wrists. Ignoring her cries of disappointment, he withdrew his cock from her and unbound her feet.

In one, smooth motion, he flipped her onto her back, spread her legs and glided into her wet and quivering pussy. Immediately, she bucked with pleasure. Grasping each wrist, he wrapped them around his neck, lifted her into a sitting position on his lap and plowed into her. He rode her rough and hard, grinding his pelvis against her clit as she screamed loud enough to bring down the house.

Finally, powerful, fantastic sensation burst upon her from every pleasure point of her body, focused on her clit as she ground out release. She sobbed, tears flowing freely, as he continued to thrust into her with all his passion. He had promised her the most powerful orgasm of her life and he had delivered. The release was nearly unbearable. Her vision blurred, her concentration moved to the spot where their bodies were joined and her hips rolled wildly.

Then Hawk stiffened as his cream filled and overfilled her before they collapsed onto his bed in a sweaty, aching pile of tangled legs and arms. Bianca shut her eyes with one final shudder and clung to Hawk's damp muscles. She never wanted him to leave her body...and as she fell into a deep and exhausted sleep, she realized she didn't want him to leave her life, either.

Chapter Nine

Hawk straightened his spine as he entered the ballroom with Bianca on his arm. After the past few weeks of heated bliss in his bed, the idea of wasting time at a party seemed cold, but it was pivotal. This night was part of proving to Bianca that they shared more than a few heated moments in bed. Still, he didn't look forward to sharing her attentions.

"Mr. Lucius Hawkins and Lady Bianca Clairemont."

For a moment the crowded room went totally silent as heads from all corners pivoted to look at the couple who had been the topic of scandalous gossip all week long. Then the murmurs and whispers began behind the elaborate fans and gloved hands.

Beside him, Bianca stiffened, though her face retained its mocking expression. Hawk looked deeply into her eyes and was surprised by what he saw. He always thought Bianca really didn't care about *ton's* opinion of her and her wild ways, but he could see by the glitter in her stare that it wasn't true. Within the startling blue, embarrassment and sadness shone. She simply covered them with that cool, distant smile that had always driven him mad because it seemed so inscrutable.

"Don't worry," he soothed just under his breath so she would be the only one to hear. "They all wish they had a fraction of the verve you do."

Bianca's laugh of dismissal tinkled around him, but Hawk sensed the shrill undertones. It was odd how a few weeks of close observation had awakened him to all her moods, even when she tried to hide them. Now the slightest change was obvious.

"Worry?" She shook her head. "You know me better than that. I never worry."

"Yes, I do know you better. I can see your anxiety in your eyes." With a gasp, she shifted under his close scrutiny.

"Hawk," she said, but her voice was low and hoarse. "Honestly, I'm fine."

A sting of disappointment worked through him. He was always reaching for a deeper connection with Bianca. Sometimes she allowed him into her confidence as she had the night he crept into her London home.

And sometimes she locked him out.

"If you say you are, I won't argue."

Her face relaxed with relief and Hawk decided not to push. Later, when she wasn't surrounded by people, perhaps he could broach the subject again. For now, he guided her through the crowd with a gentle hand on the small of her back.

Now that they'd made their entrance, only a few heads turned toward them. Though general interest had waned for the time being, each time another man looked at Bianca, Hawk went rigid. With the limited time they had left in their wager, he didn't want to share her with anyone else. To share what they had with anyone else.

Bianca slipped her arm from the cradle of his and touched his shoulder gently. He shook away his troubling thoughts with a forced smile.

"Hawk, isn't that your brother?" she whispered as she subtly motioned her head across the dance floor.

His eyes snapped up and he found himself greeted by Landon's disapproving glare. He cursed beneath his breath. For months Hawk had successfully avoided his brother by making quiet inquiries about the events he planned to attend. But Landon hadn't been on the guest list for this particular party.

Yet there he was.

Suddenly that explained Lady Lucinda Monroe's insistence that he and Bianca attend her ball. Landon had obviously demanded she invite them and that Hawk not be told of his presence until it was too late to avoid him. And Lady Monroe, social climber that she was, agreed because Landon was a respected member of the House of Lords and a powerful man.

Hawk pursed his lips as his brother arched a brow in his direction. Respected. Powerful. And too damn controlling for his own good. This night was swiftly deteriorating.

"Hawk?"

Bianca's gentle voice drew his stare away from his brother. She looked at him with a gaze filled with concern and for a moment everything else in the room, no the world, came to a halt. Her understanding expression warmed his suddenly frigid heart and he couldn't help the smile that turned his lips without effort.

"I wish I could help," she murmured.

He cupped her cheek despite how utterly inappropriate such an intimate gesture was in a crowded ballroom. "I have no choice, I'll have to talk to him. The only good thing about this night is you. The rest is pure hell."

Her expression went from innocent sympathy to wicked temptress in the blink of an eye. "My poor baby," she cooed low as she stroked her fingers along the inside curve of his arm. Even through his heavy jacket, her touch inflamed and aroused him. "I promise I'll improve your evening."

Now it was Hawk who arched an eyebrow as his troubles faded into a haze of growing desire. "Can you?"

She rose up on her tiptoes just a bit and her warm breath caressed his cheek. "Yes. I've already devised a plan."

"And what is that?" he murmured as he dipped his own head even closer. He was just a breath away from a kiss he wanted more than his next heartbeat. A kiss he couldn't take in this throng of watching eyes.

"Lady Monroe has a gazebo in her garden." She motioned her head toward the terrace door in the distance. "I have the perfect use for it. One that would shock the *ton* to no end if we were caught. But that's the fun, isn't it?"

Hawk shut his eyes as a wonderful image popped into his errant mind. Bianca on the enclosed terrace, bent over the railing as he raised her skirts and buried himself deep within her. With a few thrusts, nothing would be important but the clenching heat of her body. Not Landon. Not the wager. Not worries about his growing feelings that spurned an equally burning guilt.

Just her.

Forcing himself back to reality, he looked down at her through heavy lids. "Mmm. I would like that very much."

She took his hand with a wink that shot heat through his every vein. "Then meet me outside in a few minutes."

Hawk shivered on the brink of surrender just as Landon started making his way through the crowd toward them. With a sigh, he released her hand. "You don't know how much I long to do just that. But I think I'm about to face my brother first."

Bianca smiled with a small shrug before she turned and watched Landon stop in front of them. His gray eyes, the very same ones Hawk saw in the mirror each morning, pierced through her and focused on Hawk. And just as he had when it was his father looking at him that way, Hawk wanted to hit the man that made him feel so small.

"My lord," Bianca said with a small curtsey that would have pleased even the King, himself. "How very nice to see you."

Landon sniffed as he gave Bianca a cursory glance, then dismissed her by looking away without returning her greeting. Hawk clenched a fist at his rudeness even when Bianca smothered a laugh in her palm.

"I would like to speak to you alone," Landon said in the low, authoritative tone their father had taught him well.

Finally he found his manners by giving Bianca a curt nod. "Please excuse us, my lady."

"Meet me when you're finished, Hawk," she said with laughter still lightening her voice. "Where we planned."

Hawk managed a nod as she made her way through the crowd. He would speak with his brother alone, but Landon might not like the way it turned out. Especially after Hawk was finished with some choice words over his disregard for Bianca.

* * *

Bianca couldn't keep the smile from her lips as she wove through the crowd. Her first stop was the closest glass of champagne and then the terrace to wait for Hawk. His rage over his brother's dismissive disrespect touched her heart in places that hadn't been reached for a very long time.

Her other lovers talked in flowery language about their undying devotion when in the privacy of her bedchamber and the heat of passion. But in public, when their desire was more controlled, she sometimes sensed their discomfort with the censure of society.

Hawk was different in so many important ways. Not only did he treat her with absolute respect from the moment they stepped out of the carriage, but expected his brother and everyone else in the room to do the same.

Even if she hadn't admitted it to him when he had asked about her self-consciousness, that care for her well-being made her heart pound with nearly the same breathless desire as his hard cock did.

That emotion, the kind she had strategically avoided for so long, normally sparked terror in her breast. But not tonight. Instead, she welcomed the spread of warmth in her chest. Growing closer to Hawk, both in and out of bed, felt so right.

For a while, she wanted to savor that feeling.

She shook her head as she took a champagne flute from one of Lady Monroe's footmen, ridiculous looking in their lacy, fancy costumes. Only Lucy would put her miserable servants in pink cravats. Later, Bianca would have a laugh about it with Hawk.

She was about to make her way toward the terrace to wait for him when a hand suddenly snaked out and caught her wrist. Champagne splashed from her glass as she pivoted to see who had dared to grab her so possessively.

She expected to find her father or even Hawk holding her fast, but her heart dropped into her stomach when she found herself face to face with Everett Firth. His thin face was clean-shaven and tidy, but the desperation in his eyes gave him a haggard appearance much like he'd had when he attacked her in her home just weeks before.

But he wouldn't dare repeat that here, in front of so many people. Would he? As she glanced down at her trapped arm, she wasn't so certain.

"E-Everett," she stammered as she attempted to free her hand from his increasingly painful grip. She kept her voice as calm as she could, unwilling to show her former lover the fear he bred in her. "You startled me."

"Didn't expect to see me here, did you?" he said in a tone that chilled her very blood. "I suppose you believe I was only invited into the upper circle because of my affiliation with you."

She shook her head as she finally yanked her wrist free. As she set her empty champagne glass on a table behind her, she rubbed the red mark he'd left on her skin. When Hawk saw that…

"No, of course not. You're a powerful, influential business man." She smiled as she stroked his ego in an attempt to calm the volatile situation. "Lady Monroe would be a fool not to include you in her party invitations."

Everett's eyes narrowed to slits. "If I'm so powerful and influential, why didn't you make the wise decision to accept my proposal of marriage?"

Bianca's nostrils flared. Though Everett was keeping his tone controlled for the moment, his red face and stormy expression were drawing unwanted attention to them.

"I don't think this is the appropriate place to discuss the unfortunate problems in our relationship," she whispered, with a glare for the closest gawkers. "If you'll excuse me."

She turned, but he refused to let her. He caught her arm in a grip she couldn't escape and dragged her to the dance floor. As the strains of the waltz filled the air, he hauled her close and started to move in time with the melody.

Bianca denied her instinct to run and forced her feet to dance the steps. Making an even bigger scene wouldn't benefit anyone. People would only gossip louder about her out of control lifestyle. More rumors would only serve to drive her father's plans forward when he heard about the incident later.

Her best course of action was to let Everett have his way for a while and hope he would be finished spilling his vitriol before Hawk discovered them and broke all her former lover's teeth. For her own sake as much as the troubled man who held her so close.

"Did that bastard Hawkins throw you over already?" he hissed in her ear.

Bianca gasped as his fingers dug into her back and she was surprised that she could feel the sudden hard thrust of his erection graze her thigh. Despite his overwhelming rage, Everett desired her.

"Hawk is speaking to his brother," she answered as she tried to move away from the troubling brush of his penis. "And I'm sure he'll be back to look for me soon."

To accentuate her point, Bianca turned her head and searched the crowd. Not that she believed for a moment that Hawk was anywhere nearby. If he had been, Everett would have been nursing a broken jaw rather than dancing with her. She had no doubt the anger Hawk smothered when he'd learned Everett attacked her was just under the surface.

"Don't look for him," Everett snapped and this time he didn't try to temper his tone. "He would only make you his whore. I would make you my wife."

Hot color flashed to Bianca's cheeks at his loud, crude comment and the curious stares it brought from the other dancers.

"I will not discuss this with you here," she answered in a harsh whisper. "You certainly don't make your case by humiliating me in front of half the *ton*."

"Very well," he answered as he grasped her arm and dragged her toward the terrace. She shuffled to keep up, hoping it would look like she was taking a peaceful walk with him rather than being manhandled in the middle of a crowd that seemed intent on staring rather than coming to her aid.

He pushed the doors open and dragged her outside. A few partygoers had come out for air and most stopped to gape as Everett and Bianca moved past them. She didn't struggle as he took her down the steps and deeper into the garden. Away from prying ears.

But also away from safety. She pulled back from his grasp and backed what she hoped was a secure distance away from him.

"Now we're away from society's disapproval," Everett snarled as he pulled a cigar from his breast pocket and lit it from one of Lady Monroe's tacky Far East inspired lights that let visitors see the path at their feet. "I hope you'll do me the favor of talking to me rather than treating me like so much garbage you've thrown away."

"Everett," she said as she took another step toward the main house. Backing away gave her little comfort. Everett would certainly catch her if she ran for the ballroom. "The last thing I would ever want is for you to feel like my refuse. If I've done something to bring you to that erroneous conclusion, I do apologize."

"I don't want your damned apologies." He puffed the cigar. "I want you. I would still be willing to marry you, even after everything you've done to betray me."

Bianca's defiant nature made her want to throw that comment back in his face, but her more intellectual side reminded her that making Everett look like a fool would only bring swift and vicious punishment. Something she might not be able to avoid even with the most diplomatic replies to his ugly accusations.

"That's very big of you." She watched him pace back and forth on the path. He never took his eyes from her or let her get more than a few short feet away. "But I don't believe we would be a good match."

"Why?" He snatched her arm and crushed her closer. "You liked it when I fucked you, didn't you?"

She turned her face away from the spray of spittle that escaped his mouth and the harsh scent of cigar smoke. How had she so misjudged him? He'd never been physically abusive to her when they were together. Yet now she was terrified as a bird in a cage, waiting for the cat to open the latch.

"You were a very good lover," she admitted. "But marriage is about more than just the bedroom. You deserve more than I can or will ever give. It's best for us both to move on. Please."

The last word came out as a plea for her life, one Bianca realized she might need when Everett squeezed her arm even tighter. His eyes darkened with what could only be described as pure rage and he dropped the cigar to catch her waist roughly.

"Move on? How can I? Perhaps if you're reminded of what you've thrown away, you'll be better persuaded."

Bianca's eyes widened as Everett's hard mouth came down on hers with bruising force. As she squirmed and screamed into the unyielding wall of his lips, he dragged her off the pathway behind a wall of shrubbery and pushed her to the ground where he pinned her with his hard, fully aroused body.

She threw ineffectual punches that he easily deflected as he tore at her gown and ground his pelvis against her own. When she opened her mouth to scream for help, she was greeted by the silencing weight of his hand across her lips.

Tears burned her eyes as panic and reality set in at once. Hawk didn't know where she was or that she was in danger. And Everett Firth was going to take from her what she had struggled so long to defend and give of her own free will.

Her body. Her soul. And perhaps her very life.

Chapter Ten

Only Landon would have the arrogance to sit in another man's home, in another man's office, at another man's desk and act as if he owned the room and everything in it. Including Hawk.

His brother leaned back in his chair with folded arms. "Even you have never dared bring one of your whores out in public, Lucius."

Hawk winced at both the slur against Bianca and the use of his real name. Only his mother and brother called him that. His mother used it because she thought nicknames were vulgar. Landon did because he knew Hawk didn't like it.

"Bianca is no whore." He flexed his fingers in and out of fists behind his back. Rising to his brother's bait would be so easy, but he wouldn't give Landon the satisfaction of seeing him explode.

"Isn't she?" His brother shook his head in disbelief. "Her love life with your friend Oscar was the topic of gossip for years. When he died, instead of coming home and retaining what little respectability she had left, she dove into a long string of lovers who she has flaunted with no regard for societal standards or morality. Even her own father is at a loss for what to do to tame her. I've overheard him talking to her brothers about it at more than one event."

"What makes you think I would discuss her with *you* of all people?" Hawk clenched his teeth. "I didn't ask for your council when it comes to matters of the heart. Sometimes I doubt you even have one or would recognize true emotion if it slapped you in the face."

For a moment, it seemed his barb had hit home. Landon's face pinched in reaction and his casual posture gave way to a stiffening of his spine. "I recognize disgrace when I see it. Will that do?"

Hawk rolled his eyes. "We have the same conversation every time I'm unlucky enough to spend ten minutes with you. I tire of the repetition. Why don't you let me summarize so we can speed things along to the part where I leave and slam the door."

His brother rose to his feet. "Hawk…"

He ignored the interruption and continued in a loud, clipped tone. "You are about to tell me how disappointed you are in me. Then you'll tell me how my behavior disgraces the Hawkins name."

"And mother," Landon added quietly.

Hawk winced. His brother knew how to throw a blow without ever raising a fist. He continued with difficulty, "After we nearly exchange punches, I'll remind you that you aren't my father simply because you've inherited the title of Viscount. I don't give a damn about your disapproval."

Landon slammed a hand down on the desk with a growl of anger that resonated in the small room. "I am fully aware you don't give a damn. And yet I will continue to speak to you about it. I will *never* stop reminding you of your duty."

Hawk threw his hands up in disgust. "Why Landon? Why bother when you know this conversation will always come to the same bitter conclusion and cause a deeper and deeper rift between us?"

His brother dipped his head with a heavy sigh. When he spoke again, his voice was much quieter and filled with sober emotion. "Because you're capable of so much more. You owe your family and yourself more than to be a decadent rake who cares for nothing but pleasure and play."

Hawk drew back. In all the years they had been screaming down drawing rooms and coming close to fisticuffs, he'd never heard his brother take that tone. Or tell Hawk that his anger was about more than simple disapproval.

"I-I don't want to hear this," he muttered as he staggered for the door. He could face his brother's wrath, but not his concern. That was too much to bear.

"Bianca Clairemont is only playing a game with you." Landon's sharp voice stopped him. Hawk turned with a glare that would have frightened any other man. "She is using your appetites to attain what she wants from you. And that is the money she's lost to you in the hells. She would do the same with any man who held her vowels. *You* have nothing to do with it. If you believe otherwise, you are a fool."

Hawk's jaw twitched in rage that he barely kept in check out of respect for what was left of his familial ties. "You know nothing about my relationship with Bianca."

But in his gut, his stomach rolled. Since she'd made her scandalous bet, Hawk had often wondered about the real reason behind her sudden interest in winning her money back.

"I know more than you think. As I said, I've overheard her father talking about her several times. She's been cornered by his attempts to protect her. And you are her answer to her troubles."

"Lies!"

Landon shook his head. "By God, you're blind. Ask her if you don't believe me. Ask her why she turned to you now when she could have come to you a year ago."

Hawk frowned. Another point he'd lain awake at night pondering. But he hadn't wanted to know her reasons.

Landon stalked around the desk to stand mere feet from him. He lowered his voice to just above a whisper and said, "Or better yet, tell *her* why you couldn't come to her even though you've lusted after her since the first day you laid eyes on her. Explain the true circumstances behind Oscar's death."

The blood slowly drained from Hawk's face. Only a handful of people knew the truth about the night Oscar died. Landon was one. It had been one of the few times Hawk turned to his family for support. Now he wished he'd never trusted his brother. He'd been waiting for Landon to lord that secret over his head for years. Apparently, the time had now come.

"She doesn't need to know," he said past dry lips.

"If what you share is real, if it isn't just a way to purge your more animal desires, why not be honest?" Landon arched an eyebrow. "And demand the same honesty from her."

Hawk spun away. "Enough."

He was as desperate as a caged beast. He needed escape, he needed air. He needed to get away from his brother's pointed questions and reminders of a painful past. He wanted to lash out. To hurt Landon as much as he'd been hurt.

"I pity you. You've known nothing of passion in your staid existence. And you have never known lo-" He stopped abruptly, but not before Landon's eyes widened.

"Love? Are you saying you're actually in *love* with her?"

Hawk's heart leapt and the pounding filled his ears with rushing blood. Love. He wouldn't consider love. It had been a slip of the tongue, an overstatement he certainly hadn't meant.

"Here's the part where I slam the door," he shouted as he stalked away.

He made his way down the hall and into the ballroom. He ignored the crowd, ignored the calls of his name by friends and business associates. He needed to find Bianca. To erase his brother's accusations and pour out his turbulent emotions even as he poured his seed into her.

He slammed the terrace doors open and walked into the cool night air. He drew in a few, long breaths to calm himself as he looked around. Aside from himself, there were no other partygoers outside. And no sign of Bianca even though she promised to wait for him.

A part of Hawk's mind twitched with concern and his brother's words echoed in his mind. Her desire had nothing to do with him and everything with money. That she was cornered and using him to get what she needed to survive.

He pushed the thoughts aside. That was ridiculous. Straightening his shoulders, he hurried down the stairs into Lady Monroe's meticulous garden. The gazebo he and Bianca planned to meet in was visible in the dim light ahead. Perhaps she was there.

He was so focused on his own thoughts that it took a moment for him to realize there was a soft sound coming from the bushes to his left. With a frown, he stopped to listen. It was the muffled sound of a woman's sob.

Hawk turned on his heel and headed into the bushes to see what was going on. When he rounded the corner, he staggered to a shocked halt. In the dim lamp light he saw Everett Firth pinning Bianca down, smothering her screams with one hand as he tore at her dress with the other. Hawk's entire world went blinding red in the blink of an eye.

With a loud, hoarse cry, Hawk covered the remaining distance in one long step and grabbed Everett by the throat. In his rage, he easily lifted the other man off Bianca's trembling body and threw him across the lawn.

Hawk leapt to where Everett landed on his backside. He drew back his hand and slammed it into the other man's face. A satisfying crunch of bone met his fist, but it wasn't enough. Hawk rained punches down on the other man, pummeling him with every ounce of strength in his body.

"You son of a bitch," he cried out in a voice he hardly recognized. "You want to hurt her? To force her? You'll wish you were never born by the time I'm done with you!"

Hawk wanted to make Firth pay. He wanted him dead. And he wanted to be the one who stole his last breath.

"Please, Hawk!"

He barely heard Bianca's quiet sobs from behind him. He was far too focused on making Everett Firth cry out with pain as he raised his hands as an ineffectual shield against the barrage of punches.

Hawk reached back yet again, but before he could land another blow, strong hands gripped his collar to pull him away. Blind to his surroundings, he struggled against his captors, rushing back toward the man who dared to make Bianca weep. But the hands were too powerful and yanked him in place.

"Hawk! Hawk stop!"

He blinked as the fight began to seep out of him. His brother's voice. He relaxed his shoulders and saw two men detained him. Landon and Bianca's brother Henry Renfire. The two of them had him firmly by both arms, but each looked at him in surprise.

Hawk's gaze flitted back to Everett. The slime was on his hands and knees, spitting blood out of his puffy mouth before he started crawling away. Seeing him sent hot blood back through Hawk's system and he lunged, but the two men held him steady.

"Stop Hawkins!" Henry ordered in the tone Hawk thought was only taught to first-born sons. "Look, look at Bianca."

The mention of her name took all the fire and rage out of Hawk in the blink of an eye. He shrugged away from the men and spun to face her. She had risen to a sitting position on the grass. Her black hair tangled around her face and she pushed at her torn dress as she shivered uncontrollably from fear and cold.

"God, Bianca," he murmured as he dropped to his knees.

"Hawk," she sobbed as she leaned forward against his chest.

He tore his jacket from his shoulders to wrap it around her shoulders. Even as he held her, she continued to tremble wildly. Her breath came in long, shuddering gasps that wracked him with guilt. If only he had come out sooner. If only he hadn't left her alone in the first place.

"Take her home, Hawkins," Henry said softly.

Hawk looked up to see the two men staring at him, but this time they didn't seem horrified by his animalistic rage. Both seemed surprised by his show of concern for Bianca. Her brother was ashen-faced.

"What about-" he began

"The two of us will take care of Mr. Firth," Landon said in a cold, hard tone even Hawk had never heard before. His brother looked over his shoulder. "Damn."

Hawk peered over to where he'd left the bleeding Firth and found the bastard had managed to creep away.

Henry clenched a fist. "Just take her, Hawkins. Firth couldn't have gotten far the way you pummeled him. I'm sure we'll find him."

Hawk swiped hot tears from Bianca's face. Suddenly Firth's location wasn't important when compared to making her safe again. Making her smile return.

He gathered her into his arms, taking utmost care to be gentle as he tucked her into his embrace. "Landon, go around to the front and have my carriage brought to the alleyway behind Lady Monroe's garden wall. I'll take Bianca though the gate on the North side."

Landon gave a wordless nod as he hurried away. Hawk cocked his head. His brother had given no arguments or recriminations. That was a first.

"Come on." Henry's voice was tense. "I'll help you."

The two men walked in silence across the lawn to the gate that led to the alleyway. But Hawk could sense Henry Renfire was holding back a long list of statements.

"I shouldn't have left her alone," Hawk murmured as he shifted Bianca's weight in his arms. She rested her head on his chest. Her trembling had stopped for the most part, though from time to time she let out an enormous quiver. "I knew Firth was a danger. I should have dealt with him sooner."

"He will be dealt with." Renfire's voice was deathly calm. "And later you and I will talk about all the 'shoulds' relating to you and my sister. For now, take her home. Do whatever it is you do that makes her face light up around you."

Bianca's brother pushed open the gate and held it to reveal Hawk's carriage already waiting for them. Landon stepped out and helped Hawk carefully load Bianca inside. As he stepped up to join her, Henry stopped him.

"Whatever you do, take care of her."

Hawk looked from one brother to the next. "I intend to."

* * *

Bianca lay on Hawk's bed, looking up at the canopy above as she cursed herself for all kinds of stupidity and foolish choices. The night ran over and over in her head and she couldn't hold back a hard tremor every time she remember the sound of her gown tearing, the feel of Everett's hard, hot hands on her bare flesh. And the realization that he was going to rape her and there was nothing she could do to stop him.

"Burn this, please."

She turned her head to watch Hawk hand her torn gown over to a maid. The girl took it with a curtsey. "Anything else we can do for you, sir?"

"No. Just leave us be." He shut the door behind the girl. For a moment, he rested his forehead against the barrier. It was obvious he didn't realize Bianca was witness to his one show of emotion. To keep him from being embarrassed, she rested her head back down on the pillow and looked away.

But she'd seen his reaction and it wasn't something she would soon forget. Nor would she forget the way Hawk had attacked Firth with such hatred. He had wanted her former lover dead and would have killed him to protect and defend her if both their brothers hadn't come along to stop the fight.

"Bianca," he said softly as he came to the bed beside her. "Do you want anything else?"

She shook her head and winced at her stiff neck. "No. The bath helped a great deal, thank you. The only thing I want right now is your arms around me."

Immediately, he climbed up beside her. His strong arms went around her and he gathered her against his warm chest. She shut her eyes when he stroked her hair gently. She and Hawk had been many things to each other, but having him be her comfort was the most amazing feeling she'd experienced yet. It was something she hadn't expected, but now that she felt his care and concern, she wanted to feel protected like this for the rest of her life.

But she couldn't. It was a fool's hope.

"I'm such an idiot," she murmured against the smooth skin of his throat.

"No you weren't and you certainly aren't," he reassured her as he pressed a kiss against her temple. "How could you have known what would happen?"

She shook her head. Again and again, images from that terrible night bombarded her. "I shouldn't have let him take me onto the terrace, let alone lead me into the garden where I had no escape. He was making such a scene when we were dancing. I thought if I could talk to him alone, I might be able to calm him. And then he was on top of me and I was so shocked I couldn't breathe or scream or fight." Her voice went up with each word until she knew she sounded hysterical.

"Shhh." He took her hand and lifted it to his warm, smooth lips. "It's over now."

"Is it? Everett snuck away before any of you could do anything. Even if he hadn't, what could you do? Turn my former lover in to the constable?" She shook her head in self-disgust. "My word would mean nothing in an inquest. Not after the way I've behaved in public."

"Stop!" Hawk's voice was suddenly sharp. He cupped her chin and his eyes were alive with fire. "Never blame yourself for what happened tonight. No matter what was said or done in the past, that bastard had no right to do that to you. And he will be punished one way or another." His tone calmed and his eyes dropped. "I should have been with you. That was how this situation could have been avoided."

She raised her head at his gruff, self-abusing tone. "It wasn't your fault. You saved me. If it weren't for you I would have-he would have-"

She couldn't bring herself to say it, not out loud. Hawk seemed to sense that, for he brought his fingers up to gently cover her lips.

"We don't need to talk about it." He brushed damp hair away from her face. "But until Firth has been dealt with, you shouldn't go out alone." He smiled. "I suppose I'll just never leave your side."

She shook her head as her eyes filled with tears. It had been a long time since she'd felt protected. So long, she couldn't remember it. Feeling protected by Hawk, of all people, was even better. She could almost believe he would guard her forever.

Even though that couldn't be true.

"Why would you take care of me?" Her voice broke, but for once she didn't care if she revealed her weakness. Hawk would be her strength tonight. Showing her vulnerability seemed less frightening. "Protect me when a silly wager is what brought us together?"

He looked at her as if he didn't understand her question. "I need to."

With a tip of his head, he pressed a soft kiss on her mouth. Bianca sank into the gentle touch that was so unlike the brutal press of Everett's lips. She slipped her fingers into the crisp waves of Hawk's hair and parted her lips. She deepened the kiss with a few swipes of her tongue, drinking in the familiar comfort of his taste and letting the swell of desire rise in her veins.

Pulling back, Hawk covered her hands with his own. "No, Bianca. After what you've been through tonight, I can't-"

When she shook her head it silenced him. "After tonight, I *need* you. I need you to make me forget."

Hawk's mouth parted, but his eyes were still filled with concern and uncertainty. And desire that gave her a burst of relief. He still wanted her even now.

Bianca tilted her face closer and let her warm breath caress his lips. "You don't have to make me beg you tonight. I will without sensual torture. Please. Please, Hawk. Just touch me until I forget what his hands felt like."

He stared at her intently for a long moment. "I don't want you to beg tonight, Bianca," he whispered before his lips came back down on hers.

She arched up against him as his mouth brushed with tortuous slowness back and forth against her own. Already the bruising, painful feel of Everett's hands and mouth faded away, replaced by the hum of desire that was a permanent reaction to Hawk's lightest touch. His tongue gently parted her lips, probing delicately, even sweetly. He'd never kissed her like that before.

For a long time, she simply enjoyed his kisses. Long and soft, gentle and yet reaching for more each time he swiped his tongue against hers. Each touch awakened her uneasy body, but after some time had passed, she realized he wasn't doing more. His kisses were drugging and wonderful, but he wasn't trying to touch her or make her squirm with pleasure.

For the first time since they made their wager, he was waiting for her to lead him. She drew back slightly in surprise. Her body was how she found power after it became clear her marriage wouldn't be traditional or filled with faithful love. But in all the times she made her husband or other men beg for her touch, she'd never felt like this.

Hawk gave her more than control. His surrender was a gift. She wasn't forced to steal power. He shared it with her freely.

Because she needed it.

Tonight she wanted to feel him. To fill herself with him until there was no room for other thoughts or pains or memories.

With trembling fingers, she reached for his shirt. For the first time, she noticed a little blood splashed on the front and winced. Immediately, her gaze went to his hands. He'd thoroughly washed, but the bruises and nicks on his knuckles were a reminder of how powerful his anger had been. And how far he'd been willing to go to protect her.

One by one, she freed his buttons, spreading his shirt as she went until she pushed it off and threw it on the floor beside the bed.

Never before had she been so close to Hawk's bare flesh and free to do what she wished. She brushed her hand across his skin and a heady sense of power and pleasure filled her. His wiry chest hair bunched beneath her palm and his nipple hardened when her fingers skimmed it. He stiffened at the graze, but remained still, watching her touch him through hooded lids.

Pushing herself to a sitting position, Bianca explored further. She dragged her fingers down the taut muscles of his abdomen, running her hand along the waist of his trousers and eliciting a soft sigh from Hawk's lips.

She smiled at the sound before she dipped her head to let her tongue slide across his skin. He tasted clean and male, as good as he always smelled and she enjoyed every moment he allowed her to touch him without interruption. She caught one of his nipples between her teeth and nipped lightly. Hawk's hips surged up as he gasped and clutched the coverlet in a fist.

"I didn't hurt you, did I?" she murmured as she kissed her way to his opposite nipple.

"No," he groaned with difficulty.

She smiled against his skin. "Good. No pain tonight. No punishment. Just pleasure."

A low growl was his answer as his hands finally wrapped around her waist and bunched her nightgown in his fingers. She shut her eyes and continued to suckle his flat nipple as he kneaded her flesh gently. His touch felt so good. She wanted to lose herself in it. In him. For tonight.

For eternity.

She shivered as he slipped the thin cotton gown up her thighs. His hands were warm against the skin he exposed and her legs fell open of their own accord. He massaged the inside of her thighs, stroking his fingers in light, upward sweeps that moved him closer and closer to the core of her desire. When he finally cupped her, she shivered and her lips faltered against his skin.

"You're wet," he murmured as he massaged her sex with gentle pressure.

"You sound surprised," she gasped as he circled her clit with his thumb.

"I thought after what happened…"

She let her head fall back with a sigh when he glided a finger into her sheath. "What happened has nothing to do with you," she murmured. "You make me wild with want and nothing will change that, ever."

He tilted his head to the side and in his eyes she saw a powerful burst of emotion. Then his mouth met hers with more solid, seeking intent and she surrendered.

While he continued to pump his finger in and out of her aching body, he used his opposite hand to skillfully pop the clasps at the throat of her night shift. With one smooth motion, he pulled it over her head and left her naked to his eyes and hands and mouth. The mouth he put to good use by making a hot trail down her jaw line to the base of her throat where her pulse throbbed wildly.

She clenched her hand into a fist against his chest as he lowered her back on the bed. Her whole world was focused on his touch, on her pleasure. Like nothing else existed. She arched as he slipped a second finger into her sheath and stretched her gently. She wanted more. More of everything.

Even though she didn't voice her desires, he seemed to sense them. His lips caught the rigid thrust of her nipple and he sucked, sending lightening bolts from his mouth to tug at her ultra sensitive clit. He strummed along that bud between her thighs in time to the pulling tug of his mouth and suddenly she found herself falling, writhing, crashing into a powerful orgasm. Her hips jerked against his hand

and she lolled her head to the side with a low, satisfied moan.

When she opened her eyes, it was to the sight of Hawk staring down at her. A smile softened his face, made him appear younger and even more handsome than ever. Slowly, he withdrew his fingers and left cold emptiness in his wake as he took a position on the bed beside her.

"I don't want you to stop," she whispered as she kissed him. "I want more."

"You can have as much more as you desire," he answered just as quietly even though his eyes danced with powerful need at her demand.

She slipped her arms around him and kissed him, long and deep. He held very still and let her do what she wished, returning her kiss, but allowed her to lead them down the path of passion. It was a far cry from their normal game of domination and submission. And though in her heart she could admit she liked his overpowering sensuality, tonight was no longer about control. It had gone much deeper. For the first time in her life, making love involved more than her body. Trust was part of the equation.

And so were her emotions.

Overwhelmed, she urged him onto his back. Through his trousers, she caressed his erection, which was already hard as steel, straining against the fabric that separated skin from skin. As she locked eyes with him, she slowly opened the clasps until his cock sprung free.

She smiled as he drew in a harsh breath, then she caught his member in her palm for a long, firm stroke from base to head. His breath turned to a moan as he thrust into her hand a second time. When she let him go, he couldn't hold back a gasp of disappointment that made her smile.

"I'm not leaving," she reassured him as she carefully straddled his hips. "I just want to hold you in a much better place."

Slowly, carefully, she positioned her dripping slit above the head of his cock. She glided herself back and forth and her lips gripped at him with each pass. Hawk stiffened beneath her, biting his lip each time she clenched at him in a wet kiss. Finally she could take no more of her own torture. With a small thrust she slipped around him and took him inside her body as far as she could.

Hawk growled out his acquiescence as his hands came to grip her hips. "God, you're so hot," he moaned. "So wet."

"From you," she whispered as she squeezed him with her internal muscles. "You make me this way."

She leaned down until her hair covered his shoulders and their faces were inches apart. As she kissed him, she began to grind her hips, rotating in small circles on his cock that made her nerves and pleasure points tingle with sensation. Hawk felt it, too. He thrust his tongue into her mouth with a moan and gripped her hips until his fingers bunched.

"Sit up," she said, breathless as she leaned back.

He followed her order wordlessly. His arms came around her waist and he caught one nipple in his lips to suckle as she rode him in earnest. She bucked her hips forward and back, crying out when he lifted his own in time to her hard rhythm. He actually lifted her off the bed each time their bodies slammed together. In a heartbeat, she trembled on the edge of release and he showed her no mercy as he pounded her past that edge and over. Clasping him to her, she gave a keening cry that filled the room and shook the bed with her uncontrolled thrusts. Hawk held her fast as he, too, shouted out his pleasure and she felt the hot explosion of his essence fill her.

Their breath merged into one rasping gasp as they clung to each other, too satiated and comfortable in their tangle to let go. Bianca stroked Hawk's hair, letting her senses come back from heaven at their own pace.

Finally, he lay back down, taking her with him until she rested across his body with his pulsing cock still buried inside her. As she stroked her fingers across his body and surrendered to satiated exhaustion, Bianca realized what they had shared was no longer part of their wager.

And the game they were playing now was one she couldn't bear to lose.

Chapter Eleven

Hawk looked up at Bianca from the pile of shipping manifests in his lap. She sat on the overstuffed settee in his sitting room, her shoes slipped off and her feet tucked beneath her as she read her book with focused intent. For a moment, all he could do was stare.

In the past few days, there had been a subtle shift between them. Suddenly the lines of their wager were blurred by new emotions and desires that went beyond needs of the flesh. Bianca's walls had come down, just as he hoped they would.

But so had his own.

He was beginning to realize he didn't only like having her in his home, but his life. And now that the month of their wager was too swiftly coming to an end, he couldn't picture that life without her in it.

Just being in the same room with her moved him. Even though he knew every inch of her body, even though he could make her cry out in pleasure with just the flick of his wrist, her being so comfortable in his sitting room was what made his heart skip to a new beat.

"What are you looking at, Hawk?" She didn't even look up from her book as she smothered a smile.

It was an expression he couldn't return. Now that Hawk was getting closer and closer to her, his brother's accusations about her motives for their bargain rang louder in his ears. Some nights he lay awake, watching her sleep as he wondered if Landon was right. Was he being used?

When he didn't answer her question, Bianca glanced up at him. Her smile faded as she pressed a scrap of silk between the pages to mark her place and set her book aside. "You look troubled. Is everything all right with your business?"

He dropped his gaze from hers and wiped his emotions away. "Why did you strike your wager with me?"

His heart dropped as the color in Bianca's face faded and her lips trembled for the briefest moment. Then she pasted the smile he knew was false onto her lips.

"Silly, you know why."

He folded his arms. "Remind me."

"Very well." She sounded bored, but her eyes reminded him of an animal in a trap. "You won a very large portion of my fortune. Obviously I couldn't win it back from you in cards. I tried for months."

His nostrils flared, but he kept his expression emotionless. He didn't believe their wager was just about winning back what she'd lost. There was more to it. And today he was going to find out what.

"Is there some reason you so desperately need your money back?"

For a moment, she only stared at him, then she rose to her feet with deliberate slowness and came across the room. The shimmy of her hips was seductive, as was the smile on her face. Hawk's traitorous body reacted despite his best efforts to remain focused.

Only one thing kept his mind off the throbbing demands of his erect cock. All the trust Bianca had put in him since her attack was gone. She had returned to using her body as a weapon the instant he pushed her too far.

"Desperate?" She glided her fingers across his cheek and heat whooshed from the point of contact through his body. "There's only one thing I'm desperate for when it comes to you. And it isn't money."

Hawk's body throbbed and it took every bit of mental strength for him not to turn his cheek into her palm and pull her against his chest.

"Bianca, there must be more to it."

Her lips pursed. "Why must you ask such tedious questions? Isn't there something better we could be doing?"

He reeled away. The fact that she would use his attraction like that put a bitter taste in his mouth. It seemed to prove Landon's point exactly.

"I want to do this," he snapped. "I want the truth."

"The truth about what, Hawk?" she asked, as peevishly as he had answered.

"Why now? Why did you suddenly come to me now? And don't tell me you suddenly wanted your money back. I know you could survive nicely here in London without what I won from you. Even if you couldn't, we have been gaming together in the hells for half a year without you coming to me for a side bet."

She opened her mouth, but he cut her off. Every word he said convinced him more and more.

"And this isn't about pure desire, either. If what you wanted was me, you could have approached me any time after your mourning period was over. Something drove you to make this wager at this moment in time. Something that had nothing to do with me or our card games in the hells."

Bianca no longer tried to cover her emotions. Her face darkened to hot red and her breath came short. "Hawk." She said his name as both a plea and a warning.

He had no choice but to ignore both. "Tell me, Bianca. Tell me the truth."

She turned her face as if he'd slapped her and for a moment, she said nothing. Then her voice came, wavering and so low he had to strain to hear her.

"My father is the reason," she whispered. "He's finally grown tired of my antics."

Hawk stiffened. It was as his brother said.

She sighed, heavy and defeated. "A few weeks ago, he threatened to have me declared unfit and force my return to his home and care."

Hawk's anger was forgotten for a moment as he drew in a sharp breath. "Declared unfit? My God, Bianca, why didn't you tell me? I would have helped you. I could have intervened on your behalf."

She shook her head. "I would have been beholden to you, then."

Hawk reeled back at the sharp pain that accompanied her statement. "Beholden," he repeated in a monotone voice.

"Yes." She let her head dip down to stare at the floor. "Even if you had known the truth, you couldn't help me. Unless I'm out of his reach, he'll use the courts to bring me back under his protection. But if my fortune is returned to me, at least I have some options of recourse without becoming dependent on anyone." Her eyes glittered as they met his. "Even you."

Hawk's mouth thinned as harsh emotions overflowed in him. Anger and hurt were at the forefront, threatening to take over. It wasn't just that she'd lied, it was that she didn't trust him enough to share her troubles. She didn't think she could depend on him. Nor did she want to.

For the first time, Hawk realized how much he wished she would depend on him. That she wanted him more than she craved her independence.

"And what would you do with your money once you have it back?" he asked in a cold tone that made her wince. Good. If he was hurting, he wanted her to feel the same stab.

She hesitated. "It-it doesn't matter, does it?"

"It does matter," he said as he resisted the urge to reach out and touch her. "It matters to me since you're using me to get your fortune back."

"I'm not using you!" she gasped. Her hands came up to cover her breast, but now Hawk wondered if she was truly shocked and hurt by his accusation or just playing into his emotions as his brother had claimed.

"What will you do?" He accentuated each word.

Her frown deepened. "I'll leave," she admitted quietly. "I have friends on the continent who will take me in. My father won't be able to reach me if I'm no longer in England."

Hawk's world silently shattered around him as he stood blinking at her. "You'll go?"

For a moment her face crumpled with pain, but she shook the emotions away and bravely met his eyes. In them he saw so many tangled feelings, some the same as the tortuous ones that wracked him. But they weren't enough. Not enough to trust him. Not enough to stay.

When she reached out her hand, Hawk yanked away from her touch. He was too raw, too angry and pained to let her comfort him, even though those were ridiculous reactions. She had never promised her heart to him. He'd never asked for it.

He'd sworn he didn't want it.

He paced the room in growing anger. Anger at himself for letting his heart lead him and angry at her for using his body and his emotions to get what she wanted.

"We should have made a better deal, then. Instead of making this wager where you still have a chance of losing your fortune, you should have simply sold yourself to me," he snapped. The words were ugly, but he couldn't stop himself from lashing out.

It worked. Bianca's eyes darkened with hurt. "Hawk."

"You've earned at least half your precious money back through services rendered. Would you like to earn some more?" He hated himself for every pointed word, but the rush of pain was so loud in his ears he couldn't stop.

"Please," she whispered as she finally managed to catch his arm. Her hand held him fast and she looked up at him with teary eyes. "Don't do this."

"Why not?" he snapped as he snatched her hand away from his arm and placed it between his legs. "You've been pleading with me to let you touch me. Please me. Do it and you'll earn... what is it worth, Bianca? A few hundred pounds. From the few times you've had me in your mouth, you've been awfully good. Perhaps a thousand pounds."

"I was never trying to hurt you. I don't know how I have, but I am sorry." Her voice broke and his heart broke with it.

"Thank you, but I don't want your pity," he said softly as he turned away from the pain he'd caused her. The pain he caused himself by letting her into his life, not just his bed.

She stared at him with tears glimmering. He shut his eyes. He could no longer separate her true feelings from the emotions used for manipulation.

And he could no longer keep his own emotions from revealing too much of his heart.

A sigh shuddered from Bianca's lips. "Perhaps this wager was a mistake, Hawk. I can't cause either of us such pain any longer. I'll-I'll just need to leave."

Hawk gripped his hands into fists as he spun on her with eyes wide. "Leave? You mean go back home? It isn't safe!"

She turned away with a sigh. "No, Hawk. Not go back home. I mean leave the country. I mean go to the continent now."

* * *

Bianca couldn't believe the words had come out of her mouth with such little emotion when her heart was pounding wildly and her head spinning with thoughts and feelings. She didn't want to leave. Not her home and not Hawk. But seeing his hurt, knowing she had driven him to say such cruel things, things that were against his nature, it filled her with guilt and regrets.

Their wager was meant to be about pure carnal bliss. Not pain. And not the other emotions that clouded her judgment and kept her from maintaining control over the situation. Emotions she feared to name.

Not love. She couldn't love Hawk. She knew him too well. When she came to him, he wanted her as a prize, as his mistress. If she surrendered to that, it wouldn't keep her father from fulfilling his promise. And it wouldn't keep Hawk from boring of her. She had felt the pain of loss when a man no longer desired her. She couldn't bare it again, especially not with Hawk.

If she stayed, her life would be over. She couldn't let that happen.

So she didn't have any other choices.

"I'm sorry, Hawk," she whispered as she turned for the door.

He caught her by the shoulders and spun her back to face him. His breath was short and his eyes wild with desperation.

"You can't leave! The wager was for a month. There are still a few days left. If you leave, you forfeit the game and become my mistress."

She tried to hold back a sob, but couldn't. Tears slipped down her face as she extracted herself from his grip and gently cupped his face. "Hawk, can't you see? We're at an impasse. I cannot surrender to you. I can't lose. I will do anything to keep my father from declaring me unfit and taking away my freedom and independence."

"Even if it means letting me go?"

She jolted. The way he talked, it was as if she meant something more to him than just a month of exhilarating sex. But that couldn't be true. Hawk had never loved anyone. He wanted to win.

"Yes, Hawk. Even if that means losing you."

His face twitched as the color drained from it. "Tell me you want to stay and I'll protect you."

She shook her head. "Stay as your mistress like we agreed upon in our wager? You can't protect me legally if I'm in that position." She tried to pull away but he held her, not hurting her, but keeping her so close that his body heat enveloped her. She could almost hear the beat of his heart. "Please," she whispered. "I can't surrender and let you win this wager. I cannot bend to your will."

He growled in frustration. "And I will not bend to yours." He gave her a small shake. "I won't see you leave. I can't. I care for you."

Bianca's heart leapt at his admission. The words filled her to her very soul, but only for a moment. Then reality struck her and a small anger began to grow from the pit of her stomach. "I-I don't believe you."

Hawk yanked his hands away and stumbled back, stunned. "What?"

She set her jaw, torn between the anger alive in her and the ache at seeing him so hurt. "You heard me."

"How can you say that? You know I do not declare feelings I don't have!" he asked in a deceptively low tone.

"Wouldn't you to win a bet?" she whispered. "I know your bluffs, I've fallen prey to them before. I fear this is one of them."

"A bluff?" he repeated in an empty voice.

"You claim to care for me, but where were you in the last year? If you had come to me after my mourning period passed, I would have given myself to you. But you didn't. Our one association was a flirtation in the hells. At the end of the night, I watched you go home with your other women. Only now, when you fear you're losing control of the situation, do you claim to have feelings. How am I to believe you?"

He turned away and stumbled to the window as he ran a hand through his tangled hair. "You don't understand."

"No, I don't," she choked out. "That is why it's better if I go. Before either one of us gets hurt even more than we already have been. Before this affair becomes a bitter memory rather than a happy one."

He turned back and his eyes were haggard and wild. "Do you know how long I've wanted you?"

"Hawk, we can't-"

He ignored her. "Since your engagement party to Oscar, nearly five years ago."

Her protests died on her lips as she stared at him in utter shock. "Five years?"

"Yes." He sank into a chair as if his legs had given way. "I came home from months at sea to find my best friend engaged. I railed on him about surrendering to the siren's call of the debutantes, but from the moment I met you, I knew. My God, you could make me hard just by looking at you, just by saying hello. Getting to know you only made the situation worse. Every time I came to your home, I wanted to taste you. Every time you laughed, I wanted to bend you over a chair and make you scream beneath me."

Bianca couldn't draw enough breath. She had felt the same way. From the moment she saw Hawk, she'd wanted him. And no matter how she tried to erase those desires, they flooded back the moment he entered a room. She'd never imagined he harbored the same lust all this time.

"I didn't know," she whispered.

"Oscar did." Hawk covered his face with his hands. "He didn't like it, no matter how willing he was to share you with other men. He told me to leave you be."

He was on his feet in one sudden motion and began to pace the room. "Every time I saw him with one of his mistresses, we tangled. And every time I talked to you alone at a ball or in a parlor, we nearly came to blows."

"You fought over… over me?" Her mind reeled. "But you seemed so close."

He laughed bitterly. "Because after we beat each other to bloody pulps, we always apologized. And yet, it didn't change anything. After a few weeks we were back in the same situation. Me longing for what I couldn't have and him protecting what he didn't cherish."

She covered her sob with her hand. "I'm sorry. So sorry. I never meant to come between you."

Hawk snapped his head up and locked eyes with her. For a moment, she thought he would come to her, comfort her. She longed for his arms around her, but instead, he stayed where he was. As if he remembered she was a taboo now that he'd spoken Oscar's name.

"Don't cry. I can't stand for you to cry. Not until you know everything."

Something about his voice made her throat close. "There's more?"

"So much more," he said softly as he leaned one hand on the mantle as if it was the only thing keeping him upright. "The arguments over you escalated as the years went by. One day at our club, we started in while fencing. The argument got loud and rough and Oscar ended up stabbing me."

Bianca sank into a chair with a gasp of horror. She could think of nothing to say about that shocking news, so she murmured, "Hawk, oh Hawk!"

"It wasn't a serious wound, though it could have been had Oscar stabbed a little lower." He raised his hand to his chest as if reliving the pain. "Once he saw the blood, he felt terrible. But I planned to race the next day and was in no condition to handle a horse or a rig. So he-"

Lightheaded nausea flashed through Bianca as she raised her trembling hand to cover her lips. "Oscar took your place in the race as an apology for your fight," she whispered, barely recognizing her broken voice.

He nodded slowly. "And died when his rig flipped over. Because I wanted you, we fought. And because we fought, he died." Hawk sighed out a shaky breath. "Do you know what my first thought was when I heard of his passing?"

She shook her head slowly.

"It wasn't guilt or grief. Bianca, my first thought was that you were free. That you could be mine. And *that* is why I didn't pursue you."

Chapter Twelve

Bianca got to her feet with a wobbling jerk. Her face was so ashen gray she looked as if she would faint dead away. Holding out a hand to steady her, Hawk crossed the room, but she warded him off with a wave of her wrist.

"No. No," she gasped as she weaved toward the parlor door on unsteady legs.

Hawk's heart splintered to see her so overwrought and yet he expected nothing else. He had killed her husband, as much as if he'd shot Oscar at point blank range. Now that she knew, there was no way he could ever have a place in her life or her soul. Losing that chance burned like fire in his gut.

"Please, Bianca," he whispered as she grabbed for the doorknob. She missed the first time, but the second time she gripped it in both hands and managed to yank it open. At his plea, she came to a wobbling stop.

"Just… don't." She looked at him over her shoulder through red-rimmed eyes that seemed to see through him. "Please don't."

Hawk stared at her for a moment, memorizing how beautiful she was and trying to remember every single moment that they had shared in that instant. Then he gave her a stiff bow and backed away. "I-I apologize."

She didn't respond as she walked out and shut the door. Hawk sank into the closest chair. He had never felt so bereft. Not at his father's grave, nor his best friend's. Today he had truly lost something.

Covering his face, he tried to pull himself together. Tried to tell himself losing Bianca didn't matter. That it had all been a game, after all.

But he couldn't.

"My God, Bianca, I love you," he moaned into the muffling warmth of his hands. "I have always loved you."

* * *

Bianca took deep, calming breaths. As she entered the quiet of St. James Park, her stumbling steps slowly transformed to regular walking. Her mind was so clouded by twisted thoughts and powerful emotions she hardly remembered slipping out of Hawk's home and making her way through London's crowded streets to the serene oasis of grass and trees.

Her mind overflowed from the shock Hawk dropped into her life. Nothing she knew seemed true anymore and she struggled to make sense of the news.

Oscar had died because he'd fought with Hawk over *her*. Fought so hard they actually caused each other physical injury. Yet, their friendship had been strong enough to survive.

Only her husband hadn't. And with his death, her life changed irrevocably.

In the parlor, Hawk said the accident was his fault. She could still see the pain and guilt in his eyes and the ache in her soul deepened. But she hadn't been able to go to him, comfort him because of one truth. One painful truth became stunningly clear as she heard his confession in the parlor. Oscar's death was *her* fault.

Because she loved Hawk.

He told her he wanted her from the first moment he laid eyes on her, but the weeks they'd spent together battling the war of their wager had taught her one fundamental thing. She loved him. The very same moment his lust for her had been born, her love for him had come to life.

She loved him then and that love hadn't faded, even though she did her best to hide it away, kill it with explanations of simple desire.

Oscar sensed that in her as much as he felt it from Hawk. Her feelings had scarred a powerful friendship and eventually ended her husband's life. And yet, when she thought of the race that killed Oscar, she thanked God it hadn't been Hawk who had been in the rig that flipped. That it hadn't been Hawk whose life was cut short in one blinding, painful moment.

She covered her face with a sob. All her father's lectures about the consequences of her actions came to slap her across the face. And guilt, the most powerful expression of it she'd ever experienced, gripped her heart and soul until she sobbed freely in the middle of the square.

What did it matter if the world saw her anguish? Nothing could erase the fact that her love for another man had driven her husband down the path to his death. And nothing would change the fact that her heart still beat for Hawk and always would.

Suddenly, she felt a hand grasp her elbow. She jumped at the shock of human contact. So wrapped up in her grief, she'd honestly forgotten she was in a public place. She opened her eyes to thank the kind soul who came to her aid, but instead had to stifle a scream of shock at who held her. Everett Firth.

His face was still puffy and bruised from the beating he received at Hawk's hands not three nights before. One eye was blackened and nearly sealed shut by swelling. His nose was crooked and cut from being broken. But despite his painful external appearance, hatred and betrayal still lived in his eyes.

"Hello, Bianca," he growled.

As her heart exploded with terror, she yanked back against him, ready to scream the park down if it would bring someone to her aid. But before she could open her mouth to cry for help, the hard steel of a gun barrel pressed into her side. Everett cocked back the hammer with a smooth motion of his thumb.

"I wouldn't run or call out," he said as calmly as if he were inquiring about her health. "Give me your arm and we'll go for a stroll. No one need be hurt if you follow my instructions."

A cold sweat chilled Bianca's skin and nausea rolled her stomach as she silently nodded. At such close range, a shot from his pistol would easily kill her. If she wanted to survive, she had no choice but to let him lead her wherever he wanted her to go. At least until another escape route became clear.

They moved through the park together quietly. His coat hid the pistol so they looked like a couple taking a leisurely walk, not a kidnap victim and her captor.

Certainly no one in the park would recognize her distress and intervene on her behalf.

As for anyone else riding to her rescue, the chances were even slimmer. Hawk didn't know she'd left, let alone where she'd gone in her panicked state. Given their last encounter, he might simply believe she followed through with her vow to leave England. Her reaction to his confession had probably left him with the impression she despised him. Mostly likely, he thought she blamed him for her husband's death, not that she'd been heartbroken by her own part in the tragedy and simply needed time to process her realization that she loved him.

They reached a row of waiting carriages and with a quick glance around him; Everett helped her into one. She skirted to the far end of the vehicle in the hopes that she could put enough space between them to formulate some escape. But when Everett climbed in behind her, he pressed up against her in the seat, blocking her flight and keeping the gun trained just inches from her flesh.

"You don't have to do this," she murmured as the carriage jolted forward.

He laughed. The sound was bitter and chilling in the close quarters of the dim coach. "I'm afraid I do. You wouldn't listen to reason and you insist on carrying on with another man."

He turned to look at her. In his face, she saw the hungry gaze of a man obsessed, mad with desire and betrayal. Her heart sank. Unlike in the garden, there would be no Hawk to rescue her this time.

And if Everett wasn't satisfied by forcing her to give him her body, she might end up forfeiting much more, without ever telling Hawk how much she loved him.

* * *

"I don't understand. What do you mean, she isn't here?" Hawk growled as he braced the door to Bianca's London home open with one arm. "She isn't at my home, either. Where else would she be?"

The butler turned up his nose. "You are welcome to come in and search the house from top to bottom, sir. Lady Bianca is not at home and has not been for over a fortnight. If she had returned, I would be the first to know."

Hawk ran a hand through his hair in frustration as he searched the other man's face. It seemed he was telling the truth. But if Bianca wasn't at home... where was she?

"Fine," he barked as he pivoted back to his carriage and climbed up. "Take me to the Earl of Covey's residence," he snapped to his driver through painfully clenched teeth. "And hurry."

As the carriage pounded down the street, Hawk flexed his hands in and out of fists. When he'd finally gotten up the nerve to go up to talk to Bianca and found her gone, he thought she might have simply left his home entirely. But her wardrobe was still filled with her beautiful gowns and her lady's maid was in residence.

He hadn't panicked as he made his way to her home. After his confession, he couldn't blame her for wanting distance. It had obviously horrified her to know what his love for her had caused. She blamed him for Oscar's death.

But now the tendrils of fear and anxiety were beginning to creep into his chest. Bianca wasn't at either of their homes. She had left without escort or even a pair of gloves. And Everett Firth was still on the loose. The idea of her stumbling through dangerous city streets alone was almost too much for him to bear.

He rubbed his eyes as the carriage wheeled around a corner onto the Earl of Covey's street. Hawk wasn't looking forward to the showdown about to come, but he had no choice. If Bianca had sought refuge here at her father's home, he needed to know. And if she hadn't…well, he was going to need help to find her before she was hurt or worse.

His carriage pulled to a stop. Before his footman could open the door, Hawk flew out and up the stairs. He pounded on the door with his fist. His intuition and fears were growing with every moment and he had no time for societal rules of politeness and decorum.

"May I help you?" Covey's butler said in annoyance as he opened the door just an inch.

"Mr. Hawkins to see his lordship," he snapped out in his best no-nonsense tone. "Is he in?"

The servant's eyes flickered, as he looked Hawk up and down. In an instant he passed judgment and shook his head. "He is not in residence at present, sir, but you may leave your card."

"Not in residence my ass," Hawk growled as he pushed the door open. The servant reeled back with a cry of protest as Hawk strode down the corridor.

"Covey!" he bellowed at the top of his lungs. Parlor maids and footmen popped their heads out from various corners and the butler was at his heels prattling on as he continued to shout, "Covey where the hell are you?"

His voice echoed in the empty hallway. "Damn it, it's about your daughter's safety!"

At that, a closed door at the end of the hall opened and Alan Renfire, the Earl of Covey came into sight. His arms were folded and his blue eyes, the ones Bianca had inherited, were dark and narrow with outrage. Behind him, all three of his sons stood with similar expressions. Hawk drew in a short breath. The four men were a daunting firing squad to face, even to him.

"My daughter?" Covey snorted, as he looked Hawk up and down with the same disdainful expression the butler had used at the door. It was evident the master of the house came to the same conclusion as the servant by the way he turned up his nose. "The biggest danger to my daughter is *your* depravity."

"Where is she?" Hawk snarled as he pushed past the four men. "Is she here?"

Covey slammed the door and stalked to his desk. Bianca's oldest brother, Henry let out a laugh. "Are you saying she's finally come to her senses and left you? Good riddance."

"She didn't leave me," Hawk spat out through clenched teeth. At least, he prayed she hadn't. "She went for a walk and hasn't returned."

"But she didn't leave you, oh no," Philip Renfire taunted as he lit a cigar and puffed out a ring of smoke.

Hawk glared at the middle son before he returned his attention to the Earl. Covey stared at him as if he was a rat who had wandered into his study. Hawk he didn't care. Covey could look down on him all he liked, as long as he would work with him to find Bianca.

"By God, do you all hate me so much you can't see the larger issue here?" Hawk asked with a shake of his head. "Unless your oldest son has found him and not passed that information on to me, Everett Firth is still on the loose. I assume Henry told you he attacked Bianca at the Monroe party a few days ago. If Landon, Henry and I hadn't come upon them-" he broke off, unable to finish that thought.

The Earl's face paled and his hands gripped into fists on the desk. "Yes. Henry told me what happened. We've been looking for Firth ever since, but we haven't found him. Do you think he's still in the city? Would he dare the wrath of the Renfires and yourself for another opportunity to catch Bianca alone? He must know it's suicide."

Hawk's mouth thinned. "Henry saw him that night. I think he would agree with me when I say Firth is obsessed with your daughter. He'll do anything to regain her favor. I believe his attempt on her body that night in the garden was a twisted way of proving his love for her. If he actually took her away…" He shivered. "Her very life could be in serious danger."

"Then let *us* take care of it," Seth Renfire piped up from the corner of the room. The youngest son folded his arms with eyes flashing. Of all the Renfire heirs, Hawk felt the most animosity coming from the youngest man. "We don't need your help."

"You need all the help you can get," he said with enough heat in his voice that the room shook. "And you have no right to shut me out of the search for her."

"You have no right!" The Earl of Covey got to his feet as he slammed his palms down on his desk. "You and

163

your shameful ill use of my daughter. Treating her like she was some common whore who you can take, then discard. Don't act as if you care for her. You know nothing of what she needs."

Hawk shook his head. "I beg your pardon, my lord, but I think the same could be said about you."

A chorus of male growls greeted that statement as all the Renfire sons and their father made threatening moves toward Hawk. But he didn't back down. He couldn't.

"You hate me. I don't blame you for that. If Bianca were my daughter or sister, I would hate me, too. But if you're passing out blame for her current state, you'll have to put a part of it on yourselves." He lifted his hand as the four men began to protest. "Do you know why Bianca is staying with me? Because she came to me and proposed our current relationship. And the reason she did is because you-" He pointed to Lord Covey and the older man flinched back. "Threatened her lifestyle, her spirit, her very independence. She believes the only way to escape your well-intentioned meddling is to regain her fortune and flee the country. She used me and my feelings for her to that end."

The earl took a step back and sank into his chair with a thump. "You lie," he said softly, but in his eyes, Hawk saw he knew the truth. "I was only trying to protect her. Protect her from men like Firth. From men like you."

A surge of rage heated Hawk's blood. "Say what you will, old man, but *never* compare me to that bastard. I am in love with your daughter. I have been for as long as I can remember. I would never harm her. I would never take from her what she wouldn't willingly give. And if you won't assist me because of some ridiculous moral objection, then I will search alone."

To his surprise, it was Henry Renfire who stepped forward and took his side. "Father, I know you're upset, but I saw Bianca the night she was attacked. I believe Hawk is right about the precariousness of her position when it comes to Firth and his drive to possess her."

"Thank you, at least one of you sees reason," Hawk said on an exasperated sigh.

"Don't press what little luck you have, Hawkins." Henry locked eyes with him before he turned his attention back to his father and brothers. He sighed heavily. "I also believe this man is telling the truth. He loves Bianca. More to the point, it's evident she loves him in return. That might not be the life we would choose for her, but she seemed happy with him at the Monroe party. And he was willing to kill a man in order to protect her."

Hawk's heart jolted. Henry believed Bianca was in love with him? That she was happy? A wave of joy washed over him, bathing him in hope for the first time since he'd admitted his part in Oscar's death. If she had even a slight affection for him, he had a chance to make the past up to her. And perhaps even create a future.

The earl looked at his eldest son for a long moment before he nodded slowly. "And what do you suggest, my boy?"

"That we join forces with Hawkins to find Bianca. And argue over what to do about the two of them after we've ensured her safety." Henry turned back to Hawk. "What are your thoughts on where to look?"

He sighed with relief. From the looks on their faces, the other three men would follow Henry's lead. For now, at least, he had them as allies. "I have a few places in mind, as I'm sure you do."

"Will your brother Landon be a part of the search, as well?" Henry asked. "He was a great help the night of Bianca's attack. With his resources we could search the entire city from top to bottom in one day."

Hawk flinched. Landon *had* been helpful the night Firth went mad in the garden. He even sent word the next day to inquire after Bianca. As much as he hated to involve his brother, he had no choice.

"Yes, I'll contact Landon." He sighed. Trusting his brother wasn't going to be easy, but for Bianca he would do it.

He would do anything. Especially since her family had given him hope that maybe, just maybe, she could love him, too.

Chapter Thirteen

Being chained to a bed in one of the darkened rooms in Everett Firth's house was nothing like being tied with velvet ropes as Hawk teased her to a fever of desire. The steel binds cut into Bianca's wrists until welts rose around the metal. Everett had covered her with a blanket, but beneath she had been stripped. The terror that rose in her chest was almost overpowering. She fought to rise above it and remain calm as she awaited her fate.

She had long since given up crying out for help. Alone in a room below the main floor, no one seemed to be able to hear. Or they chose to ignore her. The latter was just as likely given how several of Everett's servants had actually assisted him in smuggling her into the house from a back entrance and securing her to the bed where she now lay.

She pulled against her chains, but as they had been the last few times she'd tested them, she found them tight and sturdy. Unlike Hawk the night she bound him to his bed, there would be no dramatic breaking of the ties.

The only way she might manage to get free would be to bargain with Everett.

She shivered at what she would be forced to give up. But certainly it was no more than what he would take when she was helpless. She didn't have to ask what he wanted from her when he stared at her with desire-glazed eyes and ran his hands over her in an obsessed fog.

With a shiver, she pushed those thoughts from her mind. Dwelling on Everett only fed her fear. To escape, she had to tamp that emotion down and depend on her wits and strength to survive. Hawk would expect that from her. And thoughts of him helped buoy her spirits.

Shutting her eyes, she pictured Hawk smiling at her. Kissing her. Holding her in his arms. To get back to him, she would do anything. Including bide her time and wait until Everett was at a weak moment.

A jangle of keys shook Bianca back to reality and she snapped her eyes open to watch Everett open the door to her makeshift cell. He spun the heavy key ring around his finger as he closed the door behind him with a cold smile.

"Are you getting settled?" he asked as he set the keys down on the table beside her bed and took a seat on the edge near her.

"I don't know how you can ask me that," she said with a laugh that surprised her with its even, calm sound. Good. Very good. Her only chance was to remain calm. "It isn't as if I had much choice in coming here."

He frowned. "Eventually you'll thank me for helping you see the error of your ways."

"You mean for helping me see my way back to you," she said softly.

She didn't want to pretend to give in too soon or Everett would be suspicious, but there was no harm letting him believe she could be turned around to his way of thinking. If he thought she was weakening to him, he might let her loose, even for just a moment. And that would be her chance. Perhaps her only one.

"Yes, exactly." He nodded. "You *do* understand what I want, what I need from you. You must see reason."

She swallowed hard. Now was the time to test her boundaries. "It would be easier to see reason if I weren't tied to a bed against my will."

He shook his head with a chilling smile. "I'm sorry, there's nothing I can do about that at present. Just because I want you to see my way of thinking doesn't mean you won't be punished for your behavior. Leaving me for Hawkins was abominable and I must make sure you never do such a thing again. You must know you are mine and only mine from now on."

Bianca's chest hurt from not breathing for so long. It seemed like it was impossible to draw breath through her terror. Punishment. Ownership. Both were dangerous concepts in the hands of a man mad with jealousy.

"What do you intend to do?" she whispered and couldn't manage to keep the fear from her voice this time.

He rolled over top of her and through his clothing and the blanket, his erection throbbed against her thigh. A wave of nausea washed over her even though she had prepared herself for what he intended to do. She knew she might not get away before he took what she wouldn't give freely. She had resolved to close her mind to what would happen to her body and look for every opportunity to escape, even if it meant pretending she loved his touch.

"First, I'm going to erase his imprint from your body by taking you," he murmured near her ear before he caught the lobe between his teeth and bit down hard enough that she winced. "And then I'm going to mark you so I'll know you're mine. And so will everyone else."

"M-Mark me?" she asked as her hands flexed helplessly in the chains. "How?"

He motioned his head toward the fire. A metal rod glowed in the embers. In horror, she realized it was a branding iron like a farmer would use on his cattle.

"What is that?" she asked. Despite her best efforts, her voice was high and bordering on hysterical.

He smiled. "My mark. I had it designed especially for you."

Tears stung her eyes and no matter how she tried to keep them from falling, she couldn't stop the flood. Rape she could stand because she could let it happen to her body without allowing it to touch her heart. Abuse she could take because it would heal and she was strong enough to keep it from destroying her.

But to be permanently scarred… marked for eternity with this man's sick crest… it was too much to bear. It would be a constant, ugly reminder that he had tried to take her soul.

"You don't have to mark me," she cried and hated herself for begging. "I will give myself to you if you want me so badly. Just leave the branding iron in the fire where it belongs."

He ran his hands up her sides and cupped her breasts through the blanket. "You've given yourself to me before, Bianca, but you still turned to another. Having my hands on you wasn't enough to remind you who owned you when another man came to call. This way you will always know who holds control over your body and so will anyone else who dares desire you. This mark is meant to make a public claim since you refuse my ring."

Bianca tried to stay in control, but the thought of being burned made her body tremble wildly. She shook beneath him, anticipating the touch of scarring steel against her flesh.

"G-Give me the ring," she pleaded. "I'll marry you. Now, here. Just don't burn me. Please."

He laughed. "You see, already you're mine and I've yet to use the brand."

With a triumphant growl, he yanked the blanket off. As he tossed the covering aside, he stared at her, mesmerized by her nudity and under the spell of his own desire. His distracted focus gave Bianca the time to gather her composure. Or at least try to.

Branding her was a terrible picture and when she thought of it, it made her sick. But Everett fed off her fears and wasn't going to free her hands if he thought she would run. The only escape was to convince him she craved his ownership, his touch and his sick desires. Including the mark that would scar her for life.

"I am yours, Everett," she whispered past the bitter bile in her throat. "If you feel you must mark me to make that claim public, then it's no less than I deserve for betraying you with Hawkins."

He brought his gaze up to her face in a slow, deliberate motion. When his eyes met hers, they were filled with cautious surprise.

"You're beginning to see reason?" he asked in a tone filled with disbelief and hope all at once.

She nodded and arched her back just enough that her breasts thrust toward him. "I am. You were right. I needed to be away from the influence of Lucius Hawkins and my own fears to begin to truly understand how devoted you are to me. How could I deny a lover so dedicated to me that he would want to make such a public claim on my body? If you need to mark me to prove that to yourself, I will let you. In fact, I'd like to help. To hold your hand as you sear my flesh with your brand."

She shivered at the imagery her words brought, but forced back her utter terror. There would be no escape without her arms being freed. This was her only chance to do that.

"The idea of the pain excites you?" he asked and by the way his erection bulged toward her, she could see there was only one answer that could help her cause.

"Yes. The moment of pain will be exhilarating. Especially when you pleasure me afterward." She felt physically ill but forced a smile. "Make me scream in agony, Everett, and then scream in ecstasy. But unlock my chains, first. Let me writhe under your touch without being bound to this bed."

She leaned forward as far as her binds would let her. "Please."

He let out a groan of desire before he caught the keys in one hand and crawled up the bed beside her. He cock pressed into her side as he bent to plunge his tongue between her lips. He thrust it in and out wetly as he slipped the key into one of the locks. The bind broke open and she slipped her hand out. A bruise was already present where the metal cut into her wrist, but she didn't care about the throbbing pain. In just a moment, she'd be free to find an escape route. Already, she glanced around for all points of possible exit.

Everett straddled her naked hips as he reached for the other lock and Bianca readied herself to knee his groin as hard as she could. But before he had a chance to slip the key into the lock, a loud bang and shouting came from outside the door.

Bianca froze in frustration as Everett's hand stilled before he set her free. She was so close to avoiding the burning brand, if only he would put the key into the other lock.

"Everett," she whispered in her most sultry voice, "Let your servants fight out their differences. I need to touch you, please."

He tilted his head to look at her and opened his mouth just as a sound echoed outside and had her soul taking flight with hope.

"Bianca!"

It was Hawk's voice, calling her from the hall outside. Screaming for her with such desperation, it actually pained her. Without thought for the consequences, she took a breath and screamed back with all her might.

"I'm here, Hawk! I'm here!"

Everett's face twisted from a smirk of desire to a mask of rage as he backhanded her with all his strength. She flew back, striking her head against the headboard. Stars lit up before her eyes, but she had enough wits about her to scream out again.

"Hawk! Hawk!"

Everett threw the keys to the bottom of the bed as he stormed toward the door. With each determined stride, he pulled the pistol he used to kidnap her out of the waistband of his pants.

The blood drained from Bianca's face. He was armed and Hawk didn't know it. If he burst into the room to her rescue, he could easily be shot and killed.

Without thought for her own safety, Bianca screamed out, "I'm here and he has a gun!"

Everett turned at the door with a howl of rage and leveled the weapon in her direction. "If I can't have you," he growled. "No one shall."

But as he pressed down on the trigger, the door splintered and flew open, striking him to the ground and sending the gun skittering across the floor with a metallic clatter.

Hawk stood outlined in the doorway. He was panting from the exertion of breaking the door down, but his eyes lit up as he saw Bianca.

"Hawk," she cried as fresh tears came to her face. "You came for me."

A little smile turned up one corner of his lips and gave him a boyish air that melted her. "I will always come for you. Nothing could stop me."

As he started into the room, Everett rose to his knees and tackled him. "Nothing but me," he howled as the two men sprawled onto the floor.

* * *

Hawk hit the ground with enough force to knock the air from his lungs, but he shoved back against Everett with every ounce of strength in his body. With a primal roar, he threw the other man from on top of him.

Hawk grabbed for the upper hand as he punched Everett squarely in his already broken nose. Firth howled at the crunch of bone, but unlike in the garden, he was ready for the attack and swung back with the lethal strength of a mad man. Hawk blocked his first punch, but the second to his gut blew the remaining wind from his lungs and sent him flying to the floor on his back.

In the background, he heard Bianca's screams of terror and fought all the harder. God only knew what Everett had already put her through. If he didn't make it through this fight, her life was forfeit. Hawk couldn't let that happen to the woman he loved.

Everett's body hit him with all his weight as he jumped onto Hawk's chest and started swinging wildly. He managed to block many of the blows, but Firth's fists hit their mark more than once. Still, Hawk didn't feel the pain. All he could think about was Bianca. Her safety, her life. With that as his motivation, he was able to get the upper hand in the struggle yet again.

A crash of splintering wood filled the air as they hit one of the chairs in the corner of the room. Hawk kept expecting Everett's servants to run to their master's rescue, but with the exception of a lame attempt to keep him out when he pounded on the door moments earlier, no one had tried to stop him. Perhaps they were as sickened by Firth's actions as he was.

The two men rolled across the floor, exchanging blows and curses. Hawk swung for Everett, but he ducked out of the way just in time and skirted out of Hawk's grasp.

He lunged for the other man again, but not before Everett swept up the pistol that had clattered across the floor and turned on him to level the weapon in his face.

"Well, well," Everett panted with a smug grin. "Isn't this interesting?"

"No," Bianca whispered from the bed. "Please, Everett, don't hurt him."

Firth never took his eyes off Hawk as he motioned for him to stand with the barrel of the weapon. With hands raised, Hawk did as he'd been ordered. His heart throbbed. The other man would shoot him and then he'd no doubt hurt Bianca even more as punishment.

"I'll do more than hurt him," Everett laughed. "I'm going to kill him. And then I'm going to do even worse to you, you lying bitch."

Hawk winced as he tried to block out pictures of Bianca being tortured because of him. He tried to forget that he would never hold her again. Never touch his lips to hers. Tears filled his eyes and he didn't try to stop them from falling.

"What a man," Firth laughed as he spit out blood. "Crying over your life."

"Not mine," Hawk whispered as he locked eyes with Firth. "Hers."

He heard Bianca gasp at the same moment Firth began to pull the trigger. He shut his eyes as he readied for the painful burn of a gunshot and then the dark peace of death. But instead, he heard a scream of pain… from Firth.

His eyes flew open just in time to see Bianca, now free from her chains, pressing a hot brand into Firth's face.

"You let him be, you son of a bitch," she screamed as the fire seared his flesh.

Hawk leapt forward. Grasping Firth's hand, he twisted it back until the wrist snapped, then slipped the gun out. Just as Everett clenched the opposite hand into a fist to punch Bianca, Hawk pulled the trigger and filled the air with the overpowering explosion of a bullet leaving the chamber and entering the man who had terrorized Hawk's woman.

Hawk didn't have to look at him to know he was dead before he hit the floor.

Chapter Fourteen

"The constable will arrest you," Bianca murmured as she leaned her head on Hawk's shoulder and rocked in time with the slowly moving carriage. "You could hang for Everett's murder."

Hawk shook his head. His life was the least of his concerns. He had almost lost Bianca and the thought of that made him shake with terror even as he held her in an attempt to comfort her.

After he shot Firth, the servants who had been hiding came down to inspect the damage. None seemed too upset about their master's demise. They'd found a gown for Bianca and promised to send the constable over after they told him their stories. Hawk had a sneaking suspicion the tales they told would leave him in the clear.

None of it mattered anymore. What mattered was Bianca and getting her home where she would be safe.

"I thought he was going to kill you," she whispered and her hand clutched at his jacket lapel.

"So much so that you apparently broke the chains," he laughed.

She smiled up at him and it was like a beautiful painting it moved him so. "I managed to grab the key with my toe and unlocked my bound wrist," she corrected him. "Don't exaggerate."

"However you broke loose, you saved my life." He tilted her chin up with one finger as he bent to kiss her gently. "And I shall never forget it. I only wish I could have saved you from all this. I'm so sorry."

"You've nothing to be sorry about," she whispered as she continued to look up at him through soft blue eyes.

"I am sorry for Oscar," he whispered and held his breath as he awaited her response.

She shook her head. "I don't want you to be sorry."

"How should I be then?"

She didn't answer except to straighten up and press a kiss on his lips. Her arms came around his back in a tight embrace as she deepened the kiss and urged him closer and closer.

"Be mine," she whispered. "Right here. Right now. Make love with me."

Without waiting for his answer, she dove back into another long, hot kiss. Her tongue gently traced his lips, then glided inside to taunt.

"Now?" he mumbled against her lips, but the protest lost its power when his hands strayed up to her buttons, seemingly of their own accord. The gown was too big and it came loose easily. His hands slid along her hot skin and she tilted her head back with a moan of pleasure that rocked him to his very core.

Even after everything that had happened in the basement room, she still wanted him. Even just the slightest touch made her hot with desire. That power was heady.

Pushing her gown open, he bent his head and blew hot air over her nipple. It puckered to a hard point as he sucked it between his lips and tugged gently.

Bianca's cry increased as she arched her back. Her fingers tangled up into his hair and she ground her hips along his thigh for relief. As he continued to tongue her nipple, he slipped a hand between her legs and rubbed her rhythmically through her gown. Her eyes fluttered shut as she rolled her hips in time with his hand.

Her chest flushed as he drew her nipple in and out of his mouth in a series of hot, wet pops. Bianca's moans came faster, more breathless as she reached for completion at his hand and mouth. He knew she was coming a split second before her cry filled the carriage. She froze in her spot, trembling before her hips thrust wildly against his hand.

She was still throbbing when she clawed at his trouser buttons. One by one, they popped free and his erection bobbed into her hand. Hawk let out a moan of his own when she stroked her palm down his length, then replaced that with her lips. She sucked greedily for a moment, sending blinding blasts of light to fill his head.

He lifted his hips up in time to her licks, reveling in her warm wetness and the moans that vibrated around his cock. Then she released him, leaving him cold for just a moment before she shoved up her skirt, straddled him and dropped down into his lap. His erection surged into heat even wetter and tighter than her mouth. Heat that still trembled from her orgasm.

"Kiss me," she murmured against his lips.

He immediately complied. She rode him as he kissed her, tasted her as he panted between thrusts. He held her against his chest as they rocked in time and brought each other closer and closer to the edge of the world.

There wasn't finesse in their lovemaking. But the desperation after such a terrifying afternoon was sweeter than anything he ever experienced. Her body clenched harder each time she ground down onto him and soon he felt her tremor in release and allowed himself to join her.

Just as he pumped hot into her, she leaned down and whispered, "I love you so much."

Her words, unexpected in the heat of the moment, made his release the most powerful of his life and he cried out long and hard as he filled her with his essence and his love.

* * *

Bianca smiled as she took Hawk's arm and he helped her down from the carriage. Warmth and satisfaction filled her every fiber as she walked up the stairs to his front door and he let her in. She said she loved him. And nothing had ever felt better. Even if he didn't return that sentiment, she needed to say it.

"Bianca," he said quietly as he led her down the hallway out of the foyer. "You should know, when I couldn't find you, I got some help. Your-"

He didn't get to finish. Before he could, Bianca's father raced out of the study and swept her into his arms to hug her. Bianca was too shocked to speak, so she simply wrapped her arms around him and felt him tremble.

"Papa," she murmured as he put her down. "Are you all right? You're shaking."

"Me?" Her father's tone was between a laugh and a sob. "I nearly lost my only daughter to a mad man today. The fact that you're here and safe makes me the best man on earth."

He touched her face briefly before he looked at Hawk. "Thank you for bringing her back unharmed." His eyes flitted to her. "You are unharmed, aren't you?"

She smiled. "I am."

"Thank God."

He ushered them both into Hawk's study. Bianca was shocked to see her brothers waiting there, as well as Landon Hawkins. Her brother's rushed forward to greet her as Landon straightened up from the mantel with a nod for his brother. As her family each embraced her in turn, she felt their relief. All of them had been terrified for her. For the first time in a long time, she felt the love of her family, untempered by disappointment or qualms over her choices. Tears stung her eyes as she took the seat her youngest brother offered her.

"Bianca, I need to speak to you," her father said as he looked down at her. His tone filled Bianca with old anxieties. Surely after today's events, he would be more driven than ever to protect her in the only way he knew how. By taking her freedom.

"Oh, please, I need a day to recover before you start questioning my sanity," she sighed with a side-glance to Hawk. He looked as nervous as she felt. "Talk to me tomorrow about having me declared incompetent."

Her father's face fell. "My actions were only meant to protect you, instead they drove you to desperation. I'm sorry I intervened so strongly."

Bianca wrinkled her brow. Her entire family was staring at her, their eyes clear of accusation for the first time in a long time. "Papa?"

"I don't pretend to approve of your choices," he said softly. "But I will no longer interfere. Your husband gave you unheard of freedom. Considering the price you paid for that freedom, I have no right to take it away. There will be no more talk about incompetence or coming home against your will."

Bianca lifted her hand to her lips with a gasp of delighted surprise. "Oh, Papa! Thank you, thank you so much. You don't know what it means to me."

Hawk stepped forward. His face was strange, pinched and pale. "I don't know what it means to you, but I know what it means to me." To her surprise, he sank to his knees before her and grasped both hands in his.

"Hawk, what are you doing?" she whispered with a quick glance at her family.

"I forfeit our bet," he said softly and the gray of his eyes seemed to surround her.

She shook her head as everything else faded. "I-I don't understand."

"I surrender the bet," he repeated slowly. "Our bet was that one of us would beg to stay at the end of our month together. I forfeit because I am begging you. Please stay with me, Bianca. Be with me, not for a month, not for a year, forever. Be my wife."

Her lips parted, but her shock was too great to say a word. All she could do was stare at him as he waited for her answer.

"Hawk," she whispered. "I don't expect so much from you. I know you-"

He lifted a hand to her lips. "You don't know, Bianca. You don't know that I love you with all of my soul.

That I never want to be without you for as long as I live. I want to marry you. Please tell me you will."

Tears slipped down her cheeks as she cupped Hawk's face in her trembling hands. She never thought it was possible to feel so much overpowering, intense joy, but there it was. Her heart felt ready to burst with it.

"I will. I will marry you."

Hawk slipped his hands into her tangled hair and kissed her long and hard. They only broke apart when Bianca's father cleared his throat loudly.

"It is customary for the potential groom to ask permission of the bride's father," he said in his most aristocratic, stern voice. Bianca clutched Hawk's arm with both her hands as she waited for the worst. "But my daughter is anything but ordinary, so I will forgive the oversight."

He shook Hawk's hand and bent to kiss Bianca's cheek. "Now we will go. You've had a trying day."

She got to her feet to hug each of her brothers goodbye. "Thank you. Thank you all so much," she whispered.

As her brothers left the room, Landon came forward. His stern expression hadn't changed since the moment they entered the room and Bianca's breath hitched. While she didn't require Landon's approval... and she knew Hawk certainly didn't... she still had hopes that the brothers could come to some reconciliation. And that she wouldn't be the cause of more strife between them than already existed.

Landon stopped in front of her, looking her over for a moment. Then, to her surprise, he smiled. She'd never seen him smile before and she realized, with shock, that it made him look more like her future husband.

"I'm pleased you were unharmed," he said with a stiff bow. "And I wish you much happiness in your marriage to my brother."

She let out a sigh of relief as she touched his arm. "Thank you."

Hawk cleared his throat as he reached out a hand to his brother. "I-" he began, as awkward as Landon. "Thank you for your help."

His brother nodded as he carefully took the offered hand and the two men shook. "No matter what, Hawk, we are brothers. You can always depend on me."

Hawk glanced at her and her eyes welled with tears at the strong emotions on his angled face. "I know that."

Landon drew back. "I'll leave you. Congratulations again. Good afternoon."

Once they were alone, Hawk closed the door and crossed the room to take her into his arms once again. She looked up at him with a smile. "You should know a few things, Mr. Hawkins, before you bind yourself irrevocably to me."

"And those are?" he asked as he swept her into his arms and carried her to the couch by the fire.

"First, I will not surrender to your will every night as I did during our wager." She touched his nose, but she hoped he saw the seriousness in her eyes. "I want to marry a partner. And while I will gladly succumb to you, there will be times when I want more."

To her surprise, he tilted his head back with a laugh that made her tingle. "My dear Bianca," he whispered as he unbuttoned her dress slowly. "I dominated you in order to win our wager. I expect we'll make love in a thousand different ways from now on. And if you don't believe me, we still have the velvet ropes upstairs. I will gladly let you tie me down and have your way with me all night."

She smiled as she urged his lips down. "After."

"After what?"

"After this." With gentle urging, she sealed their new bargain with the deepest of kisses.

About the Author

Jess Michaels always flips through every romance she buys in search of 'the good stuff', so it makes perfect sense that she writes erotic romance where she gets to turn up the heat on that good stuff and let it boil. She loves alpha males, long haired cats (and short haired ones), the last breath right before a passionate kiss and the color purple (not the movie... though that's excellent, too, the actual color). She also firmly believes that Cadbury Cream Eggs should be available all year round and not count against any diet.

Printed in the United States
62948LVS00005B/275

9 781598 361001